# Be Careful What You Wish For

# Be Careful What You Wish For

### Ten Stories About Wishes

**Edited by Lois Metzger**

*Scholastic Inc.*

New York  Toronto  London  Auckland  Sydney
Mexico City  New Delhi  Hong Kong  Buenos Aires

ISBN-13: 978-0-439-93334-6
ISBN-10: 0-439-93334-X

© 2007 "Wish Week" by Gail Carson Levine
© 2007 "That's the Way the Fortune Cookie Crumbles" by Louise Hawes
© 2007 "Our Pig, Satin" by Andrea Davis Pinkney
© 2007 "Five Djinn in a Bottle" by Liz Rosenberg
© 2007 "Black Sheep of the Family" by Patricia McCormick
© 2007 "The Fashion Contest" by Catherine Stine
© 2007 "The Reason I Will Love John MacFarlane Jr. Until the Day I Die"
   by Rachel Vail
© 2007 "Be Careful What You Wish For" by Jane Yolen and Heidi E. Y. Stemple
© 2007 "Beggar's Ride" by A. LaFaye
© 2007 "Star Light, Star Bright" by Deborah Wiles

Compilation copyright © 2007 by Lois Metzger
Foreword © 2007 by Lois Metzger

12 11 10 9 8 7 6 5                    8 9 10 11 12/0

Printed in the U.S.A.

First printing, November 2007

Special thanks to Brandi Dougherty, Linda Ferreira, Amanda Jacobs, Anne Mazer, Gina Shaw, and Roy Wandelmaier.

# Contents

# Be Careful What You Wish For

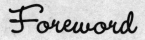
# Foreword

*Star light, star bright,*
*First star I see tonight,*
*I wish I may, I wish I might,*
*Have the wish I wish tonight.*

What if you knew—beyond a doubt—that your wish would come true? What would you wish for?

We've all heard the old stories about how wishes can backfire. A sausage can end up stuck on the end of a nose. A poor couple in a run-down hut can live in a palace for a time and end up back in the hut.

If only there were rules for this kind of thing! Rules that might include the following:

*Before you make a wish—*
*Take your time.*

There's a school in Gail Carson Levine's story where, during one week in sixth grade, every student is granted a single wish. One girl spends *years* thinking about the perfect wish. But when her turn comes, she's at a loss. What wish would be perfect enough for "Wish Week"?

*Choose your wording wisely.*

In Jane Yolen and Heidi E. Y. Stemple's story, a girl is painstakingly deliberate about *how* she asks for her wish. Then why does everything turn out exactly the way she *doesn't* want it to?

*Be flexible!*

The girl in Louise Hawes's story has been living in the shadow of her big sister. When the girl is given the power to make a wish, she can make that shadow go away. But things get tangled, and she finds herself wishing for the last thing she could have imagined.

In these ten extraordinary, original stories, you will also read about teenage genies who get stuck in a bottle; about a girl who, more than anything, wants a true friend; about a girl in a city apartment (where no animals are allowed) who desperately wants . . . a pet pig.

Maybe what they say is true—that you should be careful what you wish for. But it's even more true that when you catch sight of that bright star shining—*keep wishing!*

—Lois Metzger

# Wish Week

## by Gail Carson Levine

Your whole life, you waited for the first five school days in February of sixth grade at Pimson Middle School. Those days were Wish Week, when your most cherished wish came true and stayed true until the three o'clock bell rang on Friday.

Wish Week came once, and never again. If your family moved halfway across the country in January, you had a right to return for Wish Week. As long as you started sixth grade at Pimson, you were entitled.

If your parents didn't want to let you come back, the school sent a letter warning them not to "willfully deprive an offspring of a wish."

I wondered what the letter would say if you deprived yourself of your own wish. Wish Week began tomorrow, but I couldn't decide what to wish for.

It's not like I didn't have time to make up my mind. I've known about Wish Week since I knew about birthdays and could tell an elephant from a tiger. I'd been planning for it forever. In kindergarten I was sure my wish would be to have ice cream for every meal. I still want that, but I wouldn't waste my one wish on it anymore.

In first grade I decided my wish would be to stay up all night, every night. First grade is why they make you wait till sixth to have a wish. By sixth grade you're smarter.

Theoretically.

In second grade I was sure I'd wish to be the fairy in a fairy tale, the one handing out wishes and helping poor, unfortunate princesses.

By third grade I'd changed my mind again. I wanted to see into the future and find out everything that was going to happen to me: what I'd be when I grew up, who I'd marry *if* I was going to get married, how many kids I'd have.

Benay talked me out of that one. I remember where we were: in her bedroom, on her bed, admiring the first 500-piece jigsaw puzzle she ever finished, which her dad had framed and hung on her wall. The puzzle was of a family of koala bears. It's still there, along with a dozen more.

Anyway, she said if I could see the future, I'd find

out the mistakes I was going to make, and then I'd have to make them anyway.

That annoyed me. Why think about mistakes?

So I said that seeing my mistakes ahead of time would be useful, because I could prepare myself.

She flopped back on the bed and spoke to the ceiling. I could hardly hear her. "Tam, what if we're not friends in the future? What if we don't even know where each other lives?"

My annoyance evaporated. Benay and I had been friends since first grade, after my friendship with mean Avis Cardle had fallen apart. I didn't want to stop being friends with Benay, and to see the end coming would be horrible. In the next breath we assured each other that we'd stay friends forever, that there was no other possibility.

In fourth grade I decided my wish was going to be time travel to important moments in evolution. I'd witness the first T. rex crawling out of its shell. I'd see the tiny eohippus turn into a big draft horse. Best of all, I'd watch a person make the first fire or hear her say the first *good morning*.

My fifth-grade wish plan was to be twenty-five years old—until I thought about my oldest sister, Katherine, who was twenty-five. I'm probably richer on my allowance than she is on her paycheck, and she has to share a bedroom with two other people.

As soon as sixth grade started I got scared. Not everyone has a happy wish experience. My older sister Rori loves to draw and paint, and her wish was to be an artistic genius. During her Wish Week, she painted a self-portrait, two landscapes, and a still life. Each one was a masterpiece. But after the week ended she was back to being a talented sixth-grade artist. She was depressed for six months and didn't pick up her paintbrush for a year.

In Pimson, there's a name for what happened to Rori: post-wish trauma, or PWT. There's even a sub-specialty of psychology to deal with it. PWT therapists work here and nowhere else. Sometimes I think I'd like to be one someday. Or some kind of therapist.

For a while I thought of wishing to spend the week in a full body cast, just so I'd be ecstatic when it ended. But then I'd be miserable because I'd have missed the real wish experience.

I thought of becoming invisible. But invisibility is such a common wish that every citizen in Pimson is cautious during Wish Week. People dress in the dark. Nobody gossips or makes funny faces in the mirror. I wouldn't see or hear anything interesting.

At first, Benay couldn't make up her mind about a wish, either. She considered wishing to work on a more complicated and beautiful jigsaw puzzle than any that actually existed.

"But Tam, if the week ended before I finished, my life would be ruined."

"And if you did finish, nothing would ever be as good again."

We said together, "PWT."

Then, on Friday before Wish Week Monday, Benay chose her wish. We were in my room this time. I was sitting cross-legged on my bed, facing the poster of Christopher Reeve in *Superman*, my favorite movie. She was leaning against the fifty crocheted pillows that Dad's mom had made.

She announced, "I'm going to wish to be a prima ballerina."

It irritated me that I didn't know what *prima* meant.

"A prima ballerina is the star in a ballet company."

It irritated me even more that she knew I didn't know.

"But you've never been interested in ballet."

Benay is as skinny as a ballerina. She's tall and a little round-shouldered, and she jokes about tripping over her long fish feet. Neither of us is the slightest bit athletic.

"That's why it's good. It'll be interesting, and when I get back, I won't have PWT."

"You could have mega-PWT. What if you fall in love with being a prima?"

"Prima ballerina," she corrected me.

"Preema ballereena." I think my tone was a tad hostile. But it wasn't when I said, "You can think of something better."

She was quiet, then said in a rush, "Says the person who can't think of anything. Says the person who hasn't had a single usable wish idea all year."

*Ouch!* "Benay! I just don't think you should wish to be a ballerina."

"Well, I think I should. Stop rescuing me, Tam. You're not Supergirl."

"But it's your one and only wish, and you're—"

"You don't want me to have a wish when you don't have one."

Was that true?

No! I wanted her to have a great wish! And me to have a great one, too.

"You want us to be unhappy together," she added. "Well, I don't want to be unhappy. Wish Week is too wonderful for you to spoil." She took out her cell phone and went into the hall so I couldn't hear her conversation.

A minute later she came back in for her jacket and backpack. I followed her to the kitchen.

"Who's picking you up?" I said. Her mom and dad were both working.

"My dad."

"You got your dad to leave his job?"

She didn't answer. We stood in silence. Fifteen minutes later Mr. Bryland arrived, and Benay left without a word.

As soon as I heard the car door slam, I realized her wish really was awesome. I tried to call her cell phone, but she wouldn't pick up. I didn't leave a message. She knew who was calling.

After waiting an hour for her to call back, I got mad. She'd caused the argument. I had only tried to talk her out of a wish I thought was wrong.

Benay didn't call or IM the whole weekend. I barely slept Saturday night, so I could barely think on Sunday. Then I couldn't sleep Sunday night, either. Monday came, and I didn't have a wish.

When I got to our classroom, Benay was already in her seat right in front of mine. She didn't turn when I thunked down, twice as loud as usual.

James was in the seat next to mine, although he'd been out for a week and a half with a dislocated shoulder.

Ms. Asch, the assistant principal, spoke over the intercom. "Sixth-graders, this is the big day of the big week. I will announce each class in turn to go to the science lab. Good luck, and happy wishing!"

Mr. Bern passed out the Wish Week forms. "Use a pen, blue or black ink only. Print, no script. If you make a mistake, cross it out and continue. Remember, do not fold the form."

The form had a special chemical coating, which was why you couldn't fold it. At the top were three rules:

*You may not hurt anyone with your wish.*
*You may not hurt any animals.*
*You may not destroy property.*

The rest of the form looked like this:

NAME: _____

TYPE OF WISH
REAL LIFE: ____ (check if applies)
FANTASY: ____ (check if applies)
FANTASY/REAL-LIFE COMBO: ____
    (check if applies)

DESCRIBE YOUR WISH:
_____
_____
_____
_____
_____

SIGNATURE: _____ DATE: _____

Everybody was writing. Benay's shoulders were hunched over her page. I printed my name and signed the bottom. I wished I could have two wishes, one to know what my wish was and the other to wish it.

Ms. Asch's voice announced that room 208 could go to the lab. We were next.

"Room 209 to the lab."

Mr. Bern didn't have to tell us to file out by rows. We did it automatically, as silent and serious as worker ants. I picked up my form and took my place behind Benay. Maybe inspiration would arrive in the lab.

I followed her through the corridors. I wanted to say her wish was terrific, but it felt too late for that and too much like an apology.

In the lab we gathered around the sink. Mr. Bern took a box of wooden matches from the stack on the counter.

Jules went first. He handed his form to Mr. Bern, who struck a match and touched it to a corner of the form. The corner glowed red, curled, turned black— and then the whole form vanished. No ashes drifting toward the ceiling, no burned smell. Nothing.

Jules vanished, too. He'd chosen a fantasy wish.

Sara was next. When her form was gone, she walked out of the lab. She'd chosen a real-life wish.

I clutched my blank form. Inspiration did not come.

Three more kids went, and then Benay stepped up to the sink.

I whispered, "Benay . . . good luck. No PWT."

She faced me. "Tam?" She faced away and gave her form to Mr. Bern.

*Tam?* Tam what?

He lit her form, and she was gone.

It was my turn. I stepped back and let Katelyn go ahead of me, then Zach, and then everybody.

"What's wrong, Tam?" Mr. Bern said. "No wish?"

I nodded, wondering if he'd had other kids with the same problem.

"You'll figure your wish out." He had a seventh-grade class the next period, so he sent me to Ms. Asch's office.

There was a love seat on the wall inside her door. I put my form down and sat next to it. And sat. I went over all the wishes I'd thought of and had rejected for one reason or another.

I still rejected them.

For example, although it might be fun to be fabulously wealthy, anything I bought would evaporate on Friday. Or I could wish to be gorgeous, but it would be boring to spend five days looking in a mirror.

Sixth-grade lunch was at eleven-thirty. I was alone. If I'd wanted a hundred and forty helpings of sloppy Joe, I could have had them.

After lunch I sat again. At two o'clock I said, "Ms. Asch? Have there ever been any students who never made a wish?"

"Three."

So it was possible. I could blow off Wish Week.

After school, I took the wish form home. Before I fell asleep I tried to think of wishes alphabetically. Total failure. I didn't want an aardvark or a bear or a chicken.

On Tuesday I sat and sat again. I had to get Ms. Asch's permission to go to the bathroom two extra times so I could cry.

In the middle of the night, I woke up thinking of Benay. I wondered where she was performing. I went to my computer and searched online. The screen filled with a bio, reviews, ticket vendors. She was playing Giselle in a ballet called *Giselle* at the City Ballet in South Broughton.

She was going to get PWT, I thought.

Maybe not. I hoped she was loving every minute.

Except for the minute or two when she regretted being hateful to me.

Wednesday was worse than Tuesday. I cried openly. Ms. Asch gave me a box of tissues.

On Thursday I didn't cry. I was numb. And dumb. Nothing came.

Thursday night I dreamed I was at Benay's birthday party. Avis, my best friend in kindergarten, was there. Back then she'd been tiny and elegant, the owner of a wondrous pink hat that opened into an umbrella. I adored her.

After months of friendship, she started to call me "fatty" or "the blimp." I told her she was hurting my feelings, but she didn't care. I'd wind up crying, and she'd call me "piggy crybaby."

Eventually I stopped talking to her. Benay and I became friends, but I always felt there was unfinished business between Avis and me. In third grade her parents moved her to a different school and I never saw her again.

Until this dream. Avis kept waving to me and grinning. I kept trying and failing to talk to her.

I woke up as mad at her as if she'd teased me five minutes ago. I wanted an apology. That was my wish.

No, it wasn't. I wanted Benay to apologize.

A single apology was a tiny, selfish wish, unworthy of Wish Week. I closed my eyes and was on the edge of sleep when I thought of the expression "Walk a mile in someone else's shoes." That was it! My wish!

The glowing numbers on my clock said one A.M. It was Friday morning.

The wish form was on my desk. I turned on my desk lamp and fumbled for a pen that didn't write in fuchsia or green ink. When I found one, I put a check mark next to FANTASY/REAL-LIFE COMBO.

Then I wrote:

*I wish for the population of the earth to walk in the shoes of someone they've hurt somehow, like the person's feelings or the person's body or something the person owned. Walking in someone else's shoes means understanding that person from the inside.*

I put the date, February 6, next to my signature. That was it. A big wish wrapped around a small one. Benay would wear my shoes and apologize.

I'd give the form to Mr. Bern in the morning.

But by morning most of the day would be over in some parts of the world. I needed to start the wish now, although I doubted that I could. I clicked on my flashlight and prayed Dad wasn't still up watching a movie.

The house was silent. I tiptoed into the kitchen. Mom kept matches in the cabinet drawer that also held candles and batteries.

The faucet was dripping. I tightened it as much as

I could, since water might damage the form. I hardly ever light a match. I kept striking it too softly, and it wouldn't catch. Finally, I got it. Above the sink, I held the match to a corner of the form. The corner burned! It actually burned! A second later, the form was gone.

And the flame was scorching my finger. I dropped the match into the sink, where it landed with a hiss.

I wouldn't have to sit in Ms. Asch's office tomorrow—or go to school at all.

Back in bed I dreamed of flying shoes and boots and sandals, every kind of footwear imaginable. The dream ended with Mom shaking my shoulder. "Wake up, Tam."

I rolled onto my back. "What time is it?"

"Nine-thirty. Get up, sweetie. Avis Cardle is here."

Avis? Not Benay?

"Don't bring her into the living room," Mom said. "I'm using it."

Mom's eyes were puffy. I looked down at her feet. Her sweatpants ended in cowboy boots. She didn't own any cowboy boots, but Aunt Debra did.

"Where's Dad?"

"He went for a drive with Dr. Vogel."

Dr. Vogel had been our dentist until he pulled one of Dad's wisdom teeth—the wrong one.

"I think we're in someone's wish," Mom said on her way out of my room.

I threw on jeans and a sweatshirt. My sneakers weren't in the closet, so I pulled on my slipper socks. I tiptoed into Dad's den, where I had a view of our entryway.

Avis was holding a puffy pink parka. She was still tiny and elegant. Her hair was streaky blond with an uneven cut that was probably done yesterday. She had on an ultra-mini black skirt over black-and-pink-striped leggings. Her feet were in my ratty black sneakers, which didn't look ratty on her. She'd exchanged the laces for pink ones arranged in a complicated pattern, the left foot done one way, the right another.

Her clothes declared her the coolest sixth-grader on the planet. But her face was sad. Really sad.

"Avis?"

"Tam? Can I come in?"

"Sure." I led her into the den. "Give me your jacket."

I draped the jacket over Dad's desk chair. She put her pink messenger bag on the floor, brushed cat hairs off the sofa, and sat on its edge, feet together.

"How are you doing?" I said, dropping into the recliner.

"Okay. Tam, I'm sorry." She started to cry. "So sorry." She wept into her hands. "So sorry."

I couldn't help smiling. Her apology soothed a spot that had been raw for six years.

"I wouldn't"—she was crying too hard to get the words out easily—"have teased you"—sob—"if I'd known"—sob—"how much . . . you liked me."

Huh? That was what my shoes told her? "Not how bad I felt?" I asked.

She nodded. "And how bad . . . I made . . . you feel." She took her hands away. Tears streamed down her face. "But I don't . . . think . . . anybody's ever . . . liked me as much as you did."

Probably not, if she treated other people like she'd treated me.

"You *admired* me." She hiccuped. "I wish I'd known."

I hadn't kept it a secret. As soon as I had the thought, I felt sorry for her, sorry she couldn't tell that I liked her. Loved her. I didn't know it then, but I did.

If she still couldn't tell when people liked her, she wouldn't know who her true friends were. I sat next to her and rubbed her back.

"Thanks." She reached into her messenger bag. "Here. I brought this for you." She pulled out her umbrella hat.

It was too small for my head, but I turned it around until I found the button under the brim. I pressed it, and the spokes shot up. One of them was bent.

"A souvenir," she said.

"Thank you."

"Tam? Could we be friends again? We could go shopping. . . ." She stopped. "You hate to shop."

"Usually."

She made pigeon toes with her feet in my sneakers. "We don't do the same things." She took off the sneakers and held them out to me. "Was this your Wish Week wish?"

"Partly."

"Everybody at my school wishes we had Wish Week." She produced a pair of pink clogs from her messenger bag and put them on. "Will I remember this?"

"Maybe a little, but it'll be fuzzy." Only the wisher remembers her wish in detail.

"I have to go now." She put on her jacket and left.

I went back to my room. Inside the door was a pair of white ballet slippers. I had Benay's shoes!

She'd been mean, and *I* had her shoes. My own wish wasn't being fair.

I held the slippers in my hands. What if I put them on and learned Benay didn't want me for a friend anymore?

Better to find out from her shoes than from her lips. I sat on the floor to put on the slippers, which fit perfectly, even though Benay's feet are two sizes bigger than mine. I crisscrossed the laces and tied them halfway up my calves.

Putting them on didn't make me feel any different. I stood and tried to go up on the stiff toes. I wobbled and stepped. With the step came understanding.

I had to talk to her!

But I couldn't. Mom and Dad wouldn't let me go to South Broughton alone. Even if I sneaked out and biked to the train station, I didn't know the train schedule or how to get to the City Ballet. And there wasn't much time. It was eleven, and Wish Week ended at three.

Still, I had to try. I started for my door.

And I was in the wings of a theater. There were dancers onstage, but it seemed to be a rehearsal because only a few people were watching, and there was no music. The dancers formed a tight semicircle, facing away from me.

They drew back. Space opened between them, and I saw Benay, crouching, her face tragic. She exploded out of her crouch and began to leap and whirl. Her leaps were impossibly high and long. She stretched her arms behind her—nothing round-shouldered about her now—and ran into the arms of a male dancer. He danced her around for a minute, then set her down. She curtsied to him and left the stage, coming at me in four enormous bounds.

I saw the moment she recognized me, when her face went from tragic to glad. I grinned back, the happiest I'd felt in months.

"You came!"

"Sorry I made you doubt your wish. It's perfect."

A man's voice yelled, "Benay!"

She yelled back, "Be there in a minute." She lowered her voice. "Sorry I was nasty, but when you didn't like it . . ." She shrugged.

"I know." With my first step in her shoes, I understood. When I'd said I didn't like her wish, it had collapsed on her and seemed a bad, stupid choice. Worst of all, she'd felt silly for wanting to be something as showoffy as a ballerina.

"I decided to do it anyway," she said.

"You were brave."

"How did you get here?"

"Benay!" the man yelled again.

"Coming! I have to go. I'm not performing tonight, but they don't know that."

"Later," I said.

She ran back onstage.

I stepped closer to see her better.

And was in my room again, wearing my sneakers. I checked my watch. Eleven-thirty. Three and a half hours were left, but my wish was over. The best parts had been watching Benay dance and seeing her smile when she noticed me.

I turned on the TV, channel surfing. When I hit CNN, I heard a newscaster say, "An age-old adage comes true today as people far and wide walk a mile in someone else's shoes."

On the screen was an outdoor square. I saw palm trees. And people hugging. People yelling at each other and then hugging. People crying and people laughing, and people doing both at once.

The camera panned down to everyone's feet. Some women were wearing men's shoes, miraculously shrunken to size. Some men were wearing women's shoes. Women in suits wore plastic sandals. Men in suits wore running shoes.

I jumped up and down, my heart racing. This was my wish, too!

The scene shifted to a newsroom. A newscaster said, "We've just received confirmation from the United Nations. The phenomenon is worldwide. Shoes everywhere have been switched. From pole to pole people are reaching out to estranged loved ones, former friends, and current enemies."

The crawl read, "Developed countries pledge record sums to fight hunger and disease."

The newscaster continued, "Experts place the source of today's events to Pimson Middle School, where the annual sixth-grade Wish Week is in its final day."

There was school! First the building, then the hallways, where seventh- and eighth-graders were laughing and crying and yelling and hugging, just as the people in the tropical square had been.

A reporter interviewed Ms. Asch. A man I didn't recognize stood behind Ms. Asch's chair, his hands on her shoulders, smiling down on her.

She spoke into the reporter's microphone. "I wouldn't know if we've ever had a wish with this much impact." She laughed. "I wouldn't remember."

Back in the newsroom, a newscaster was grinning through tears. "Police stations all over the country report no crime since shortly after one A.M. this morning, Eastern Standard Time. No violence of any kind."

I was grinning through tears, too.

"Our foreign correspondents report the same. No violence. Military operations have been suspended in hot spots around the globe. The Grim Reaper is taking a vacation."

I lay back on my bed. I'd come up with a good wish, a great wish, a wish worthy of Wish Week.

At four P.M., someone in Detroit was attacked and robbed. Still, the entire month after Wish Week was extraordinarily peaceful.

I kept the umbrella hat. Mom and Aunt Debra got along better than before. Benay began to stand like a prima ballerina, back straight, toes turned out. I'll always remember her dancing, and we're friends again, closer than ever.

And neither of us got PWT.

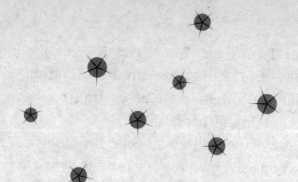

# That's the Way the Fortune Cookie Crumbles

**by Louise Hawes**

"Not one step closer!"

I put down my math book, which isn't all that hard to do because I hate factoring anyway. I listen through the wall between my bedroom and Lacey's.

"I told you before," my sister yells. "Get out of my sight!"

Normally, the only person Lacey screams at like that is me. But I'm right here, sprawled on my bed with *Adventures in Sixth-Grade Math*, half a bag of spicy taco chips, and the remains of the Halloween stash I've had for nearly three weeks now. I get up and peek out my door.

"You have to stop sneaking in here!" Lacey tells

someone I can't see. "You have to leave me alone." Her voice breaks like she's tired of shouting, pleading—like she might even be getting ready to cry. "Please! Put down that hammer!"

I'm down the hall and inside her door in about two seconds. I brace myself for the worst, breathing fast, looking around the room for a dangerous stranger. I can feel my knees tense, and I'm ready to leap ... but to where? Lacey straightens and stares at me. She's standing by her bed, a loose-leaf binder in her hand. And that's when it dawns on me. I've made a splendid, shining fool of myself—it's just a *script*.

My sister is an actress. It's all she's ever wanted to be. Since she was a tiny kid she's been pointed, straight as an arrow, toward Broadway. Not Hollywood. Broadway. "Movies aren't art," she tells me all the time. "Movies are getting it right after five hundred takes." Lacey always looks serious when she talks about the stage, like she's someone much older than sixteen.

So here I am, ready to save my big sister's life, and all she can do is laugh. It's not a small chuckle, either, not one of her you're-so-misguided-and-amusing laughs. It's Mount Saint Lacey, arms folded, head thrown back, tears running down her cheeks, whole body erupting with these deafening oh-my-God-I'm-the-sister-of-a-moron cackles.

When she finally stops, I sit on her bed. "So," I ask her, "what's the new play about?"

She brightens. "It's a murder mystery," she tells me. "I'm trying out for the part of the last victim. I get killed in the third act."

"And that's good?" It's pretty hard to be mad at Lacey when she's happy. She loves rehearsing and knows she's awesome. Not in an obnoxious way. Just this quiet sureness that makes her light up all over. I'd give a lot to be that sure of anything.

"It's a *great* death scene," she says, as if that explains it all.

"Cool." Even when she was my age, they used to send Lacey up from the middle school to play kid parts in the high-school plays. "If that's the role you want, you'll get it. You're the best. Everyone knows it."

Lacey smiles and shrugs. "We've got a transfer student from Manhattan this year." Whenever Lacey talks about the city, she never calls it New York, always Manhattan. The way she says it, it sounds like Marrakech or Timbuktu, some exotic place in another country instead of a forty-minute train ride from our house in New Jersey. "Tanya is the daughter of Elaine Beldon." She stops, breathes deeply, puts one hand on her chest. "THE Elaine Beldon."

"Elaine Beldon?" I glance at Lacey's wall, wondering

if the name she's just whispered like a prayer belongs to one of the famous faces in the huge photo collage over her bed.

Lacey points to one of those faces, halfway down, surrounded by a cloud of jet-black hair. "Elaine played the wicked aunt in *Come Darkness*," she explains. "And the dying mother in *Sooner than Later*." Now she's counting on her fingers. "And the crazy sister in *Sailing into the Sun*. And—"

"She's big, huh?"

Lacey is so worked up, she's glowing. "The *biggest*," she says. "And Tanya looks exactly like her. Same tiny waist, same hair and eyes." She sits down beside me on the bed, and puts the script in her lap. "If she acts the way she looks, this may be a real contest."

"There's nobody you can't outact, dead or alive," I tell her. My sister not getting a part she wants would be like rain falling up or my dad skipping dessert. Impossible.

Lacey takes a long, hard look at me. Even though I do my best impersonation of a smiley-face bumper sticker, she sees right through it. "What's with you, Spence?" she asks. "Did somebody just outlaw chocolate?"

I scooch out of range of her X-ray vision. "Let's just say," I tell her, "that today was not my finest hour."

Lacey frowns. "Bad, huh?"

"Lousy," I say. No, that's not right. "Completely awful," I correct myself. Then I replay school in my head and settle on the only description that fits. "The Temple of Doom."

She puts her arm around me. "Tell your big sis."

How can I? How can someone who always gets what she wants understand someone who never does? Lacey kind of floats through life, blond and beautiful and adored by all. She gets A's, friends, and boys without even trying. She's got her learner's permit, a perfect figure, and her own phone. Me? I have red hair that's never met a comb it couldn't break, and a shape that's—well, shapeless. I have a bike that pops its chain twice a day, two good friends (three if you include Alfred, but cats probably don't count), and the only time a boy's ever spoken to me outside of school was when Terrance Branson called me to get Winona Siler's phone number.

So if you're thinking that my sister and I live on two different planets, you're right. Still, I like sitting on her bed, talking to her, better than sitting on mine, wrestling with square roots. "First," I say, "I spent ten minutes this morning trying to open my locker."

Lacey: nothing.

"Then I missed every single question on my math homework."

Lacey: still nothing.

"They served chipped beef for lunch."

Lacey: looks a little sympathetic.

"And the entire sixth grade laughed at my career path."

Lacey: "Career path?"

"We had a special assembly on the future," I tell her. "And everyone who sat in the front row had to say what they wanted to do with their education. I only sat in the front because Cara and I were late, and those were the last two seats left."

Lacey nods.

"Everyone seemed to know just what they're going to do," I say. "Paleontologist. Heart surgeon. Architect. All the good ideas were used up by the time they got to me."

"So what did you say?" Lacey strokes her script, like she's telling her character she'll be right back.

"Well," I say, "I thought about telling them I hadn't decided. But then it came to me, and I just blurted it out. 'Cosmetologist,' I said. 'I want to be a cosmetologist.' That's when the whole place cracked up." Even now, in Lacey's room, I can hear those sneaky giggles starting in front and spreading likes waves to the back of the auditorium. "And I still don't see what's so funny!"

Mount Saint Lacey is laughing again, rolling on the bed. "Spence," she says, when she's got herself under control. "Do you know what a cosmetologist *does*?"

"Sure," I tell her. "A cosmetologist studies the cosmos—you know, stars and planets and black holes."

Lacey looks at me from under her thick, movie-star lashes. "Cosmetologists are *hairdressers*, Spence." She's still trying not to laugh. "You didn't tell everyone you're headed for the stars. You told them you're into mud packs and the layered look."

"Oh," I say. "No wonder Erin Pulley asked me if her bangs were too short."

"Hey, not a biggie." My sister lifts my chin up with her hand, like I'm about two years old. "By next week, someone else will have made an even dumber mistake, and your little slip will be ancient history."

"Thanks," I say. "Thanks a lot." I feel the tears start up in my eyes.

Then she makes it worse. "Besides, you've got more than public humiliation to worry about. It's Friday. MY Friday. We eat where I say tonight."

"No!" My taste buds shrivel up on themselves. "You wouldn't!"

All of Lacey's big-sister compassion has vanished. Her voice is smug and evil. "Oh, yes, I would. Mom says we have to take turns, and you dragged us to Olé last week. You know how Dad hates those clown hats in the drinks."

"They aren't *clown* hats," I tell her. "They're sombreros. And everyone in our family likes the food at Olé." Now it's my turn to pour on the guilt. "It's not like one of us is highly *allergic* to eating there and wants to barf all over the table as soon as she sits down."

Lacey folds her arms. "*A*," she says, "you're not allergic to Chinese food. And *B*, you know Lang-Po's is my favorite restaurant in the medium-price range."

I cross my arms, too, and try not to think about the greasy-fish smell that comes out of the kitchen every time a waiter pushes through the door of Lang-Po's busy dining room.

"For your information," Lacey goes on, "Mom loves moo-shu pork and says that the emperor's wontons are bites of heaven."

It's true. Everyone in my family is crazy about Chinese food. Everyone but me. Another day, I might be a good sport about this, but today has *not* brought out my inner Girl Scout. "You can all go without me," I tell her, hearing how whiny and dumb I sound but not being able to stop. "There isn't anything you or Mom or Dad can do to make me eat a single thing on that stupid menu. I'm staying home." I stand up and head for Lacey's door. Before I leave, I turn around and put my hands on my hips. "Case closed. Period. Finito. THE END."

Lang-Po's is even more crowded than usual. Around a small lacquered table in the back of the dining room, Dad sits opposite me, and Lacey and Mom face each other. "What happened to democracy?" I ask while everyone's studying poster-size menus. "Why didn't we take a vote on coming here?"

Dad is the only one who looks up from his menu. "This isn't a democracy," he says. "It's a family." His voice is slow and matter-of-fact, like he's reading a grocery list. "Lacey is dictator this week. Then Mom. Then me. It will be your turn again next month."

"If I live that long." I glance at the giant smiling Buddha on the wall in front of me, then scan my menu, hoping desperately there's a new section, Kids Who Hate Chinese Food. There isn't.

Just when I'm wondering if it's too dark to walk home, Dad winks at me. "How about you and I share the mango pudding?" he asks.

Sharing food almost always makes it taste better. At Lang-Po's, the puddings come with or without chocolate sauce. (I know. Why would anyone order them *without*?)

"Can we start with dessert?" I ask.

Everyone laughs. After that, things get easier. Of course, we don't actually start with dessert, but we end up having a pretty decent dinner. I hold my breath while I chew, and I make it all the way through to the pudding. Dad asks for extra chocolate sauce, so I hardly taste the mango underneath. By the time the waitress brings out fortune cookies, we're talking and cracking jokes.

"Okay," Mom says, when she gets her cookie. "I was late to work today, my intern never showed up, and nobody read the report I worked on for three weeks." I'm a little sorry now for the way I acted earlier. It sounds as if Mom is at least runner-up for Most Depressing Day Since the World Began.

Except, it turns out, *she's* fighting back. Instead of opening her cookie, she hands it to Lacey. "I am *not* going to get stuck with the fortune fate plans to unload on me," she says. "Pass to the right, gang."

It has taken me one-millionth of a nanosecond to figure out that passing to the right means I'll get my sister's fortune. I hand over my own cookie to Dad and take the one Lacey passes to me. If it was meant for her, how bad could it be?

We always read our fortunes out loud. But when it's my turn, I can't. I just shake my head and put the purple paper I've unrolled in the middle of the table. It's different from everyone else's. Not just because it's purple, but because it's got gold sprinkles in the paper and the letters scrawled across it aren't written in English. They're Chinese!

Dad calls over our waitress, who has pretty, almond-shaped eyes and dark hair. She laughs and says she's fourth-generation, and even her parents can't read Chinese characters.

Finally, after Dad and Mom have decided to trade their fortunes (Mom's says she will travel soon, and Dad's says he'll find himself surrounded with laughter), and Lacey has announced she wants to keep hers (it says she will excel in her chosen field), Lang-Po's owner, Mr. Cheng, comes to our table to look at mine.

Mr. Cheng must like his own food. A lot. He is broad and round. He takes out his glasses and studies my purple paper. Then he tells us, "This is a mistake." He turns to me, apologetic. "I will get you a cookie like the rest."

"Please," I say, "can you read it, anyway?" I have a delicious suspicion that my luck's about to change.

"This is not a cookie fortune," he tells me. He smooths out the paper and puts it in front of me. "This is a temple scroll."

"Temple scroll?" Dad looks as surprised as Mr. Cheng. "Isn't that what Buddhist monks give you when you visit them?"

Mr. Cheng nods. "Yes, indeed," he says, looking pleased that Dad understands. "This is the old Chinese way to tell the future."

I feel shivery all over. "What does it say?"

"It is a poem," the restaurant owner says. "A poem in Chinese does not rhyme like a poem in English. Words dance and make a picture."

"What picture?"

Mr. Cheng picks up the paper again. "This says that the future is like a bird in a nest," he reads. "Sometimes rain falls on the bird, and the bird hides under a wing. But sometimes the bird calls out the sun with song. This scroll is like a bird's song. Your next wish, no matter how big, will come true."

"Wow!" Lacey looks really impressed, and everyone else looks amazed. Mr. Cheng heads back to the kitchen, and suddenly I remember about wishes. In fairy tales, they almost always give you more than you bargained for. Like King Midas, who wanted everything he touched to turn to gold, and everything did—even his own daughter.

"Be careful, Spence," Lacey tells me, as if she's read my mind. "When I played the Little Mermaid and I wished for legs, it cost me my voice."

I check under the table. "I've already got legs," I say.

"I don't think we need to worry about Spence

wasting her wish on a prince." Mom looks around the table. "There are lots bigger things to wish for if we've only got one shot."

*We?* Does this mean we're a democracy, after all? I fold the purple paper into a tiny square and hide it in my pocket.

"I think asking for world peace makes a lot of sense." Mom seems pleased with herself. "I mean, how could *that* backfire?"

"Now, hold the phone," Dad says. "This is Spence's wish, and I don't think she should have to worry about world peace or anything bigger than her heart's desire."

"Thanks, Dad," I tell him. I'm really glad he said this, because all the things I've been considering wishing for are pretty selfish.

"Come to think of it," he adds now, winking again, "my fortune says I'm going to travel. Maybe you'll wish that our whole family wins a golf getaway at Pine Ridge?"

"Dad!" Lacey's taking my wish more seriously. "Spence should wish for something long-term, like a new house for all of us. With bigger bedrooms for Spence and me. And a home studio. And a sauna." It's like she's reading this stuff from a list in her head. "We'll need a workout room, and . . ."

It flashes through my mind that I could wish for

Lacey's figure—no workout required! But maybe I'd rather have her phone. Or her report card. Or her sureness. Let's face it. I should probably just play it smart and wish I had my sister's life.

I know better, though, than to waste the purple scroll on the first things that come into my head. Or my family's heads. They may think this is a big joke, but what if it isn't? "Listen up, everyone," I say. "As the Official Wish Maker, I have decided to take a week to think things over."

"A week?" Mom looks as though world peace shouldn't have to wait another minute.

"Yes," I tell her. "Just in case this is for real. I don't want to make any mistakes."

"Good," Lacey says, surprising me. "No point rushing into something like this. It takes time to think about colors and extra features." She stops in the middle of her own fantasy, eyes wide. "Like what if we ended up with no high-def?"

The next day, all I can think about is the scroll in my pocket and the wish I'm going to make. It's probably not really, truly magic, but still . . . At breakfast, I study Alfred, curled up like a fat, contented crescent roll on the kitchen windowsill. I consider wishing that no cat or dog would ever be homeless. Then I think about the wise, smiling Buddha on Lang-Po's wall and decide my wish should include people, too.

I'm feeling pretty good about this wish—until I notice the T-shirt Lacey is wearing. It's got a zipper down the front. Well, not a real zipper. It's a silver drawing and it looks great against the black background. ZIP IT, white letters say above the drawing, I ALREADY KNOW I'M A 10. Suddenly, I don't care about homeless people as much as I did a second ago. More than anything, I want to be able to wear that shirt. I want to be pretty enough, cool enough, funny enough.

When Cara calls after breakfast and asks me to go to the mall, I say yes right away. I get my bike out of the garage and meet her at the corner. We ride over to Music Mania (my chain only pops once) and find the newest album by Cara's all-time favorite band. We take turns listening to tracks through headphones. For the next hour, I forget about fortune cookies, and world peace, and lost kittens. Then the only person who could snap me back into wishing mode walks into the store.

Lacey and her three friends don't even notice us. I don't wave or call out to them, but I watch Maya, Rachel, and Shelley follow my sister to the movie section. When all four of them start giggling, they remind me of the girls in my class who hang around the gym after school and wait for boys' soccer practice to end. They always stand right by the locker-room door, so they can "accidentally" be studying the bulletin board when the team comes out.

Sure enough, a few minutes later, a group of senior guys walk into Mania and head for the video games section, which is "accidentally" next to the movie section. I can't help it; I almost make my wish this minute. Because—honestly? There's nothing I'd like more than to have just one boy look at me the way all those seniors are looking at Lacey. She's like a disco light, or a white star that's fallen right in front of them, and they can't take their eyes off her. Who wouldn't want to be gazed at like that?

I reach into my pocket and take out the purple paper—then remember how I've decided to wait a week. I put the paper back, grab Cara by the shoulders, and tell her about the cute sneakers in the shoe store we passed on our way here. She gets this happy, eager look on her face. World peace, homeless people, and animal orphans have just been saved by my friend's hunger for hightops!

It goes like this for the rest of the day. Even after the weekend, when school starts, I'm still obsessing.

I come pretty close to making my wish as soon as Lacey gets home on Monday. I'm doing my homework, and I hear a noise below my room. I go downstairs and open the door between the kitchen and the garage. Neither of my parents is home, so the big, empty space for their cars is the perfect spot for my sister's hula-hoop practice. She and a bunch of girls from the drama club are learning to spin giant flashing hoops to music. They've turned out the lights, and I stand there, watching them. Until someone drops her hoop and laughs, it is just about the most beautiful, otherworldly sight I've ever seen. Like comets orbiting in a night sky, the hoops spin round and round, leaving tracks of silver and blue and gold. Who wouldn't wish she could do something so amazing?

On Tuesday, I nearly spend my wish again. As I'm walking (slowly) to math class, I catch myself imagining that my name is on the honor roll posted in the hall outside the principal's office. Mom likes to tell people that Lacey was on that list every single semester she was in middle school. I don't think Mom means to make me feel bad, but because my name's never been up there even once, let's just say my heart doesn't exactly sing when Mom starts boasting like that. Who wouldn't wish to be someone her mother could brag about?

Today is Wednesday. As soon as I walk in the door,

Mom tells me a secret she's been dying to share. "Guess what your father is giving Lacey for her birthday?" she asks.

"I don't understand why people make such a fuss over birthdays," I say. "I mean, it's not like Lacey has a choice about turning seventeen."

"A car!"

"A *what*?"

"A hunter-green convertible with leather seats, and a GPS navigational system, and remote entry, and a power console, and . . ."

I'm sure there are lots more accessories and features, but I don't stay to hear the rest of the list. Instead, I go up to my room to sulk. I know I should be happy for my sister. But all I can think of is that, next month, she'll be able to load up her car with friends and go out to movies and parties. And she definitely won't need a baby sister going along for the ride.

I take the fortune-cookie paper out of my pocket and study it. I stare at all those graceful black letters that mean a bird can keep the rain away with its wing or bring out the sun with its song. I'm picturing myself with a driver's license and a new green convertible when I hear the front door open.

From up in my room, I hear Lacey's footsteps stop by the hall table, then go into the kitchen. I wonder if Mom will be able to keep her secret or if I'm going to hear my sister race up to her room and get on the phone to tell all her friends the good news. But after Lacey comes upstairs, instead of gleeful giggles, I hear the last thing I'm expecting—sobs.

My big sister is crying alone in her room!

At first, I'm sure it's just another script, and I stay put. Soon, though, the sobs get bigger and harder. They go on and on. Worse, still, I don't hear any dialogue at all. Would a character in a play ever cry so long, without talking?

Now I'm outside Lacey's door, and the crying is louder than ever. When I knock, it doesn't stop. Maybe she didn't hear me? I knock harder. I know what it's like to cry like that. When Alfred was hit by a car and Mom took him to the vet, I cried all night. Even after Dad told me my cat was going to be okay, I still couldn't stop. The whole time he was talking about how Alfred was already eating and doing his rollover trick, I kept right on sputtering and shaking. It was like my mind heard him, but my body wasn't getting the message.

"Lace?" I open her door and peek in. "Are you all right?"

She's lying on her stomach on the bed. Her head is buried in her arms. Those awful sobs keep on coming.

"Lacey?"

When she finally looks up, she's not surprised, not angry. It's like she's so full of misery, there's no room for anything else. Long, runny tear tracks streak both cheeks; her movie-star lashes are clumped together; and she really, really needs a tissue for her nose. I go into the bathroom and come back with one. She takes it from me and sits up, her shoulders shivering in a baby-bird way that makes me want to hug her. I sit down beside her. "Tell your little sis," I say.

"The . . . auditions were today." She stares at the tissue in her hands. Her hair falls over her face. It's as if that beautiful, bouncy light has been sucked right out of her.

My stomach feels strange. Or is it my heart that's gone all tight in my chest?

"Tanya wasn't good," Lacey says.

"But—"

"She was *great.*" Lacey has that faraway look people get when they're replaying things in their heads. "She was *better* than great." A huge sigh, part sob. "It was like she was made for that part, and no one else could measure up." Sniffles, and another sigh. "I didn't even come close."

Rain is falling up. My big sister has lost her

confidence. It feels wrong. No, it feels horrible. I want things back the way they were, with Lacey always winning, always the star I aim for, the place I want to be.

"Is it—is it for sure?" I ask.

"Ms. Hartford didn't announce the results, if that's what you mean." Lacey's eyes are red and hopeless. "She didn't have to." Her voice is throaty from crying. "She'll post the cast list tomorrow morning, but I already know who got the part."

"No, you don't!" I take the purple paper out of my pocket. I unfold it, so the bird in the poem can stretch its wings. I don't even think about boys or flashing hoops or honor rolls. "I hereby wish that my sister, Lacey Stayson, the greatest actress in the universe, gets the lead in the next school play."

Lacey looks at me, stunned. In fact, I'm kind of surprised myself. After all that careful planning and worrying about homeless people and animals, I've finally made my wish.

"Spence!" My sister sounds as if she's going to start crying all over again. "What have you done?"

To be perfectly honest, I'm not sure. The room gets quiet, and the two of us just sit here on Lacey's bed. Are we waiting for magic to happen? Will we feel it, if it does? Then, after a few seconds, what I feel, sudden and warm, are my sister's arms around me. She grabs me as if I were a life raft, and holds, holds, holds.

"Oh, Spence, I love you so much." She's still sniffling, and I can feel my neck getting all wet, but I don't mind. "Even if that silly fortune cookie doesn't work," she says, "you're the most incredible, best sister anyone, anywhere, could ever have!"

You know what? Even though I complain about how hard it is to be her sister, I feel just the same way about Lacey. So if this story were to end right here and now, with me and my sister hugging the daylights out of each other—well, that would be just fine with me. Of course, if it could end with Lacey coming home tomorrow and announcing that Ms. Hartford took into account that Lacey's a senior and Tanya's only a junior, so she decided to give the part to Lacey, that would be even better. And if this news were to make my sister so happy that she gives me her zipper shirt, and teaches me to hula-hoop, and promises to take me along on her very first drive in her brand-new car—well, *that* would be a wish come true!

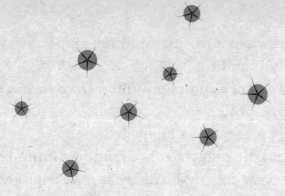

# Our Pig, Satin

**by Andrea Davis Pinkney**

Here are four things I know about pigs.

1. Pigs are cute.
2. Pigs have curly tails.
3. Pigs do not oink. They squeal.
4. Pigs are soft.

Here are three more things I know about pigs:

5. I wish I had a pig.
6. I wish for a pig every day.
7. I have been wishing for a pig all twelve years of my life.

I am very clear on my pig wish.

I don't want a toy pig from the grab-bag machine at Coney Island.

I don't want a cutout of Wilbur from the *Charlotte's Web* movie poster.

I don't want a Miss Piggy doll.

The plastic piggy bank Grandma Ginny bought me last year for my birthday is *so* second grade. (I didn't want that pig, either.)

I want a real, live, curly-tailed, soft, squealy pig. I want a barnyard animal.

This is why my pig wish can never come true. I don't live in a barnyard. I live with Mama and Grandma Ginny on Lawson Avenue in the Clifton apartment complex, in the Bronx. In New York City. In the middle of traffic and concrete and construction, and with a subway station two blocks from home.

As I sit at my window and watch the blue Bronx night sweep her cape over my neighborhood, my wishing is so, so strong.

I can see my pig so clearly in my own wish-bubble.

If I had a pig, she would be a girl pig. If I had a pig, I would name her Satin. After all, pigs *are* pink.

"Satin," I would say softly. "You are *so* special."

Satin would be my friend. She would adore me. And I would sure love her.

"Lisi!" When Mama calls me from the kitchen, my wish-bubble is busted. "Lisi, child, come away from that window. How many times do I have to *tell* you?"

Mama doesn't let up. "*What* are you doing?" she wants to know. "Don't waste your time daydreaming."

"I'm not daydreaming," I call back. "I'm *wishing*," I say quietly.

I try to go back to my wish-bubble. I imagine Satin curled up at the foot of my bed, lying on her side as she sleeps, her gentle pig snores rising up as soft little hisses.

Mama calls back again, louder this time. "Lisi—is your homework done?"

"Yes, Mama."

"Did you lay out your clothes for tomorrow?"

"*Yes*, Mama!" I call.

"What about your shoes? Are they by the front door? You're always looking for your shoes when it's time to leave for school."

Thoughts of my pig are fading as fast as the dusk. And with all of Mama's mouthing, I can't get those pig wishes back.

"Mama," I snap. "My shoes are ready!"

Mama comes from the kitchen. She sees me upset and softens. She hugs me from behind. She rests her chin on my head. Together we look at the lights along the avenue coming up brighter and stronger in what now is a black night sprinkled with neon. Mama says, "You're still chewing on that pig wish, aren't you, child?"

I don't answer, just nod.

"Lisi, you know good and well this is no place for a pig. We can't even have a cat in this building."

I twist free from Mama's hug.

"You shouldn't waste time wishing for something you can't have," says Mama.

That's when Grandma Ginny comes home from choir practice. "I hope this isn't a pity party, 'cause the good Lord frowns on those who feel sorry for themselves." She tosses her keys onto the dining-room table.

Mama says, "This is no kind of party. But Lisi is sitting on her own pity pot, wishing for a pig. *Again*."

"What about that gold piggy bank I bought you, Lisi?"

"It's almost full," I say. "And besides, that's not a real pig. I want a *real* pig."

"Humph." Grandma shrugs. "If I was twelve and my piggy bank was almost full, I'd be wishing on a *real* chance to go to college—and I'd be thankful that I had a pig full of money to start off my college savings account."

I hold off from rolling my eyes. "Whatever," I say.

"Whatever?" says Grandma Ginny. "I'll tell you *whatever*. This is 462 Lawson Avenue, in the Clifton apartment complex, in the Bronx. There are no real pigs within fifty miles of here. Unless you count Brother Jamal's Bar-B-Q Shack over on Tyson Boulevard, where Brother Jamal and all his people claim the pig's feet are gen-u-ine swine."

Grandma Ginny cracks up at her own stupid joke. Mama's laughing, too.

I suck my teeth hard. "Does this look like a comedy lounge to you? 'Cause I'm not laughing."

Mama lifts my chin. She looks at me straight on. "Lisi, honey, Grandma's just trying to keep it light. She's right—there are no real pigs around here."

"All right then," I say. "Welcome to my pity pot."

This is all Grandma Ginny needs for more of her *keep it light*. "Child," says Grandma Ginny, "if you sit on the pity pot too long, you get a ring around your booty."

Mama and Grandma lock fingers in their own version of a high five. This is all so funny to them.

Now the night is black. I press my forehead to the window. From the fourteenth floor we watch the who's who on Lawson Avenue.

"There's L.T.," Mama says, as the old man everyone calls Little Timmy—or L.T., for short—crosses the intersection with his cane. His hat is cocked to one side, and like always, he's dressed like it's worship Sunday. He hobbles slowly in the crosswalk, making his way across the street, long after the light has changed. Somehow the cars in our neighborhood know to let him pass at his own pace. Nobody beeps, or hollers, or curses Little Timmy along.

On the far corner, where Lawson meets Gagne Avenue, Grandma Ginny spots a kid we all know as Z-Boy. "That child is one of those entrepreneurs," Grandma Ginny says. "Always looking for a way to make a dollar."

Tonight Z-Boy has set up a card table and is shuffling cards. He's playing music and getting people to crowd around. And somehow, he's collecting their money. There are mostly big boys and eager men gathered near Z-Boy. But tonight they are joined by Wanda Bright, the best-dressed lady in the whole Bronx. She's not playing cards, just watching other people lose money. "Look," I say, "there's Wanda Bright!"

Grandma Ginny folds her arms. Mama folds hers the same way. Tight as can be. Together they let their disapproval be known. *"Uh, uh, uh."*

Grandma Ginny says, "That woman is too much of too much."

"A clotheshorse of the worst kind," says Mama.

I am quick to defend Wanda Bright. She gives new meaning to the word *style*. She is a fashionista with flash. Even though the buildings along our street block the stars, Wanda Bright twinkles in her own way.

I have never met Wanda. But everyone on the street knows her. She has many nicknames.

Sparkles.

Fringe-maker.

Bangle-shaker.

And my all-time favorite—Bling Lady.

There is no doubt how Wanda came by these names. She is always wearing something flashy. Wanda is big on shoes and bags and bracelets. And she loves labels.

The thing is, though, people think Wanda's a fake. Tonight we are too high up to see Wanda closely. We *can* see that she's wearing red. And I can spot her Louis Vuitton bag a mile away. Even from fourteen floors above, she shines.

Grandma Ginny says, "Look at her parading around like she does. That designer stuff is no way real. I know where she works. No way does she make the kind of money where she can afford anything with a label that isn't cut in half. What a phony-baloney."

Mama agrees. "She is a walking advertisement

for knockoffs, strutting like she's some runway model."

"The runways of make-believe fashion," Grandma Ginny is quick to add. "I've seen enough of this mess." She sniffs.

She and Mama go back to the kitchen.

People can say what they want about Wanda. I can see the clothes, but I can see *her*, too. Her confidence. I wouldn't mind confidence like that! I watch Wanda walk up the avenue, adding her twinkle to the starless city night.

Mama is back soon with a dish towel and the piggy bank from Grandma Ginny. She rests the dish towel on my shoulder. "Time to help dry," she says.

"Why'd you bring the bank?" I ask.

"Grandma Ginny forgot to mention that the good Lord also believes that faith can bring a miracle. Have faith, Lisi," Mama says. "Things have a way of working out, maybe not in the ways you'd expect." She hands me a penny. "Make a wish, then drop some copper."

I close my eyes and plunk the penny into the bank.

Mama says, "It's better than a ring around your booty."

I can't help but smile.

"I'll dry the pans. You take the plates," I say. And together we go to the kitchen.

The next day I spot Wanda Bright.

I am sitting out on the steps of my apartment building when I see her coming down the street. Today Wanda is *dressed*. She is wearing a killer leather coat, sleeves scrunched just right at the elbows, bangles jangling like a subway samba band, dark, dark sunglasses, and shoes with the classiest heels I've ever seen. The whole outfit is topped with just the right amount of bling—diamonds in the shape of a *W* hanging on a thin chain around Wanda's neck. There are earrings to match.

The bling is *workin'*.

Wanda sees me looking at her. When she's close enough, I say, "Hey."

"Hey yourself," she says. I can't see her eyes. The shades are so dark.

"What *are* you looking at?"

I blink. Wanda Bright is more beautiful up close. I have never seen teeth that white. And, oh, her skin. It is the smoothest, darkest chocolate ever. Along with the shades and the shoes, Wanda has her Louis Vuitton slung over her shoulder. My eyes go from those white-as-white teeth to the chocolate-chip complexion to the Louis Vuitton pocketbook.

Man, the bag is *nice*.

"Is that the real thing, or a look-alike from the street?" I ask.

She takes the bag off her shoulder so I can get a better look. "Touch it," is all she says.

I feel the leather. It's grainy. But it's smooth, so smooth.

"Now," says Wanda, "you tell me."

I tell her straight. "That is no fake."

She smiles. "This is the best Louis there is. The Satchel, they call it. And, honey, it's more real than reality TV."

"I believe you," I say.

"Everybody in the whole neighborhood thinks I'm a big fake. They don't know. I'm careful with my money. I spend it wisely. I know a good deal when I see one."

"I can see that your stuff is real, and it's beautiful," I say. "But I wouldn't care if it was real or not."

Wanda tilts her shades, so I can see her eyes. Kind, friendly eyes. And she's looking at me like nobody else has ever looked at me. Like I wasn't just some kid who got yelled at to do homework or go find her shoes or get off the pity pot. "You wouldn't care if my clothes were the real thing, would you?" she said.

"No. *You* are real, that's what's important." I stand up from the curb. Somehow it doesn't seem right to sit when talking to Wanda. "My name's Lisi—Lisi Jones. I live here, in the Clifton apartment complex, building B-36."

I am not wearing any designer anything. I'm walking around in my same old, same old: jeans and a T-shirt with a pig on the front. I do have a little gold belt, though, with a pink rhinestone pig for a buckle. I can tell Wanda likes the belt. She keeps checking it out.

She offers me one of her slender hands. The bangles make their happy noise. She has a French manicure, of course. "I'm Wanda," she says.

"Wanda Bright," I say.

We shake hands, once, firm.

"You know my name?" Wanda has rested her sunglasses on the top of her head. Her hair is cropped and natural and beautiful.

"*Everybody* knows your name," I say.

"True," Wanda giggles. "I mean, I am a *bright* spot in the neighborhood."

Wanda gestures toward my belt.

"I like bling, too," I say.

"And you like pigs. I can see that."

"I like pigs more than anything! All my life, all I've ever wanted is a pig! My own pet pig." I let it drop. What a silly thing to say to somebody like Wanda Bright, who has far more important stuff to think about.

"We have some things in common, Lisi J," says Wanda. She flips her shades back down over her eyes and says good-bye.

Weeks go by before I meet up again with Wanda Bright. Before then I watch her from my window, coming and going with all her real-as-real-can-be designer clothes. And Wanda's got enough bling to open her own diamond district.

I still spend most of my nights wishing for a pet pig, arguing with Grandma Ginny about the pity pot, and putting more pennies in my piggy bank, trying to keep my faith alive. Every night when a penny falls into the bank and clanks against the other copper in the bunch, I whisper the same prayer. "I wish, wish, wish for a pig. A real pig."

Then, one day when it's too hot to sit in our apartment, I take to the steps of the Clifton apartment complex, building B-36. And here comes Wanda Bright! She is walking the sidewalk like it's opening day for a fashion show collection. She is greeting the neighbors like they are editors from *Vogue* magazine and *Harper's Bazaar*. And of course, Wanda is stylin'.

She picks up her pace when she notices I'm on the steps. She's glad to see me.

"Lisi J! Hey, girl," she says.

I don't recognize any of her clothes. They all look new. But the Louis Vuitton bag—the Satchel—is the same as always. This time Wanda settles herself next to me on the steps. "How you been?" she asks.

I'm glad to see her, too. "I'm hangin' in," I say. "You look good."

Wanda checks her reflection in the bank door next to where we're sitting. "I *do* look good, don't I?"

That's when I notice that something's pushing from inside Wanda's Louis Vuitton. The leather is bulging, and there's motion on the clasp.

"Lisi, I have found the perfect accessory to complete my whole fashion statement. I've got a—"

I know exactly what Wanda's done. I've seen ladies riding the number 6 train down along Lexington Avenue with the same thing. I guess Wanda's secret before she can even say it. "You got one of those little dogs to carry in your purse," I blurt out. "Wanda, you have gone all the way on the fashion trip now," I say, all smart.

Wanda answers me quick. "Girl, you think you know *everything*."

"Those dogs are called Yorkies, right?"

"Yes," Wanda says, "the *dogs* are called Yorkies, Ms. Smart-Thing. But a Yorkie is no kind of original fashion statement. I got me a—"

"—Chihuahua," I interrupt.

Wanda stomps one foot like she's frustrated.

Without saying anything else, she gently unclasps her satchel. I put my face closer to the open bag. When I see what's inside, my heart pounds more than a midtown Manhattan jackhammer. I can't believe what I'm looking at. I wonder if my mind is playing some kind of bad trick on me.

Wanda leans closer. "She likes it when you pet her under her chin." Her voice is low, like she doesn't want to draw attention. Wanda's talking on the q.t., and I see why.

Inside Wanda Bright's Louis Vuitton satchel, there is a pig! A baby pig! A piglet, dressed as well as Wanda! The pig is wearing a small houndstooth coat with a nubby black fur collar. There are tiny sparkly hoop earrings clipped to the pig's ears. The earrings have a matching necklace—a diamond-encrusted *P* on a chain. "Even a pig needs some bling," Wanda says. And to make it all the more sweet, there are sunglasses angled between the pig's ears.

The piglet presses her snout up out of the bag to greet me.

I swallow once and blink. All I can say is, *"Oh, oh, oh . . ."*

"You want to hold her?" asks Wanda.

I nod so fast. Now I'm thinking, this is a *good* dream, not a trick. Wanda opens up the collar on the pig's coat. The pig looks up at me with eyes that are happy to meet a friend. I set the baby pig on my lap. Wanda puts her bag in front of the pig so nobody can see what I'm holding.

"Hey," I say quietly as I run the back of my fingers along the little roll of skin under the pig's chin. The piglet's tail is a teeny letter Q, done in the cutest cursive. And oh, is she soft. A bundle of cotton candy. Just like I knew a pig would be. Her coloring is white-pink. Like a cloud when the sun is setting. She is more beautiful than any toy from Coney Island.

"Where'd you get her?" I ask Wanda.

Wanda adjusts the pig's earrings that are coming loose.

"It took me a while, Lisi J," says Wanda. "I have connections all over, even in the world of pigs. And after we had our little conversation, I knew I had to get her." She is now wearing the best fashion of all—a little knowing smirk, like she and I have a special secret between us. "You see," says Wanda, "just like you, I have wanted a pig for as long as I can remember."

I have to keep from squealing. My insides have gone from jackhammer to all-out happy.

"And," Wanda continues, "I do *not* believe in depriving myself. And I do not believe in depriving *you*. Because, Lisi J, I think you're real, too."

I didn't know what to say. It was like getting a bonus wish I hadn't even seen coming.

"And why in the world would I get a Yorkie or any dog for my purse when I can have a one-of-a-kind fashion statement like this?"

"But how did you get the owners of the Clifton apartment complex to let you have a pig?" I want to know.

"Are you kidding, girl? Nobody *let* me do anything. If anyone ever knew I had a pig, I'd be out of this apartment complex faster than you can get to a sale at Saks. You know the rules—no pets, no radios, no menus."

I nod. I know all the rules.

"And," says Wanda, "it goes without saying—"

We say it together: "No pigs!"

Now Wanda is petting the piglet.

"I'm looking for the perfect name," she says.

I don't have to think twice. "Satin," I suggest.

"Satin . . ." Wanda lets the name settle for a moment. "Nice, Lisi J. Real nice."

I could swear the little pig smiled right then.

"Satin, you are *so* special," I say.

Wanda says, "Satin is our piglet, Lisi J."

"*Ours?* Really?"

This has to be a dream. I just know Mama and Grandma Ginny are gonna call me any minute and ruin everything—*"Wake up, sleepy head! Get off the pity pot! Is your homework done? Where are your shoes?"*

But Mama and Grandma Ginny are no place in sight. I'm wide awake, hanging out with Wanda Bright—and *our* piglet. Satin.

Then my doubt comes back quick.

"Share?" I ask. I want to make sure I'm hearing right.

Wanda nods once. "Yours and mine."

Then, even without Mama or Grandma Ginny messing up this beautiful moment, I realize how impossible the whole thing is. I'm sad to say it, but I do. "I can't share a pig. Mama will have a cow if I bring home a pig."

Wanda's smirk is still there. "Girl, who says you have to bring her home? Satin can live with me. All you have to do is help me love her."

I am quietly thanking Grandma Ginny's good Lord. "So this is a wish come true for you, too?" I ask Wanda.

"You know it," Wanda says.

Somehow I get the feeling she's not just talking about the pig.

Wanda gently settles the piglet back down in her purse. There is enough of an opening for the pig's snout to poke out for air. Wanda positions her Louis Vuitton on my shoulder. She says, "When we're out together, you can walk Satin—in the Satchel, of course."

"With the little piggy shades on, of course," I add.

"You got it, girl," Wanda confirms.

She flips her own sunglasses down over her eyes and reaches into the pocket of her jacket to pull out a spare pair of shades. She hands the shades to me. "They're Dolce & Gabbana."

They're the darkest, coolest shades ever, with tiny bling-bling rhinestones along the sides. I see my reflection in the bank window. I look good.

Little Timmy is crossing the street in front of us. He is stopping traffic, like always. And, like always, no one seems to mind.

And here comes Z-Boy. Today he's selling some kind of candy. "Hey, Wanda," he calls. "Want something sweet?"

"I got something sweet already," Wanda shouts back.

And so, on a hot and happy afternoon, Wanda Bright and I, heads high, walk up Lawson Avenue in the Bronx, in New York City, with our pig, Satin, and enough bling to outshine the sun.

# Five Djinn in a Bottle

**by Liz Rosenberg**

"You got us into this. Now get us out!" fumed Inan. She'd turned herself into a flickering column of flame, in delicate shades of red, cerulean blue, yellow, and white. *Even at her angriest, she was still beautiful*, Shayma thought, *unlike me*. Shayma was a djinn who could take on the shape and spirit of a dog. Her mother said Shayma was beautiful, like an Irish setter, but Shayma didn't believe her.

All five teenage djinn were in the same Enchanter's Study Circle, a kind of high-school AP course. And like mischievous high-school kids out for a joy ride, they'd been caught just as dawn was breaking, crumpled in a tangled heap by the splashing fountain in the mortal's yard, having that moment landed and fallen off his best flying carpet. And if a mortal caught sight of djinn in the light, they were easily captured. Now the tiny djinn were stuck in his bottle until he'd made his three wishes or released them out of the goodness of his heart. The latter seemed highly unlikely.

It was worse than maddening to be caught by such a creature, thought Shayma, it was embarrassing. What would her mother say? She and her sister, Mao-ming, would be grounded for a century, at least.

"If you hadn't pushed me," Nikolai said to Inan. He folded his wings and glowered. Even while Inan was frowning at him, Shayma knew he was still mesmerized by her shimmering flames.

"I didn't push you; I fell!" Inan exclaimed. "And I wouldn't have fallen if Shayma hadn't been so clumsy and tripped me!"

Shayma snorted. "I told you there wasn't enough time. I smelled the mortal, remember? I knew it was almost light out. But Ghul kept saying it was pitch-dark. We should've known better than to listen to him!"

Instantly, Shayma regretted her words. Was it Ghul's fault that he didn't know the difference between night and day? Ghul was the color of night, almost the same color as the midnight blue glass of the antique perfume bottle they'd been crammed into.

"Enough blaming!" said Mao-ming quietly. She was the eldest. In school and out, they listened to her. "Think! The mortal might be spiteful and wish us in here for a thousand years. It's happened! Can you imagine that? A thousand years in this"—she shuddered—"soda bottle."

A thousand years. By then they would all be middle-aged. The thought cast a pall over all five of the djinn. Even Inan stopped burning and resumed her usual form, coffee-colored skin and dark hair. She chewed at one pretty pink fingernail.

Then, before they knew what was happening, they were flung from one end of the tiny bottle to the other, up and down and at a slant. Nikolai and Ghul, both flying djinn, took wing at once. But the three female djinn landed in a heap at the bottom of the bottle.

The mortal's voice boomed from above. "I HEAR YOU DOWN THERE, SHOUTING AT ONE AN-OTHER. I NEED YOU TO CONCENTRATE ... ON ME! YOU WILL BE SERVING ... ME! NOW BE QUIET WHILE I THINK ABOUT MY WISHES." He shook the bottle once more for good measure, and this time Shayma clunked heads with Nikolai.

"Maybe he'll want to take another peek at us," Mao-ming whispered. "Maybe he'll open the bottle a little."

"Then we're free—*whoosh*!" Ghul shouted.

"Shhh!" The other four put their hands over Ghul's lips.

"Sorry," he mouthed. "*Whoosh.*" He said it more quietly this time.

They sat there a good long while, waiting, not saying a word. But the bottle didn't open, not even the tiniest crack.

"The mortal may be stupid and coarse," said Mao-ming. "But he knows better than to let us out."

The mortal placed the bottle on his marble mantlepiece, with all his other trinkets. Were all these things, including this bottle, stolen? Mortals didn't usually come into magic carpets legally. He did possess some wonderful things, Shayma thought, remembering the marvelous carpet, crimson and blue silk, hand-knotted fringe, and how it flew like the wind, faster than Ghul, faster even than Nikolai at his most daring. Oh, it had been almost worth this terrible trouble to feel the night sky rushing against her face!

*Yes, and the feeling of Nikolai leaning so close to you*, Mao-ming thought at her.

Shayma winced. Sometimes she forgot her sister could read her mind.

"I can shape-shift," said Ghul. He often said things like that, out of the blue.

"Duh," said Inan. "We know!"

"I mean," said Ghul, "maybe I can shape-shift and scare him off."

"From inside this bottle?" said Nikolai. "Get real."

Shayma eyed Ghul thoughtfully. *Exactly how small could he get?* she wondered.

"Not small enough to escape," said Mao-ming. "If that's what you're wondering."

Sometimes Shayma wished she could snap her brain closed against her sister, like a box.

"True," said Ghul, and his mood grew visibly darker. He looked like a pool of black ink. "However," he added, "I can change the shape of the bottle we're in."

Inan leaped to her feet and threw her arms around him. "You can?" she cried. "That's brilliant!"

But Mao-ming warned, "The mortal still has to open the bottle."

"Based on all the empty bottles lying around, he opens bottles all the time," Inan said. "Beer bottles. Yoo-Hoo bottles. Milk of magnesia bottles. Just turn into one of those."

"But we're up on his mantlepiece. He'd wonder how a bottle of Yoo-Hoo got up there."

"He wouldn't wonder—he'd just drink it, the greedy thing," Inan said.

"Maybe," said Mao-ming. "It's worth a try, anyway."

*And you had to hand it to Ghul*, Shayma thought. He turned their cobalt blue glass prison, with its intricate mosaic inlay work, into a bottle of fine wine. The mortal's servant carried it down to the basement, apologizing for having mislaid an expensive bottle of Lafite-Rothschild, 1954.

Shayma wished she could be clever like that.

But within the hour, the mortal had wished them back: "I KNOW YOU'RE HIDING SOMEWHERE! I WISH YOU WERE BACK IN MY BOTTLE, RIGHT HERE ON MY MANTELPIECE, WHERE I CAN KEEP MY EYE ON YOU!"

Wishing, thought Shayma, was like being thrown into a whirlwind, or churned inside the ocean. You scraped against things and came up gasping for air. It might be easy for a mortal to make a wish, but that didn't make it easy for a djinn to grant it.

"TRYING TO ESCAPE, WERE YOU?" The mortal's laughter was like the hissing of a hundred snakes. "YOU BRATTY KIDS CAN'T PUT ONE OVER ON ME!"

*But they had, hadn't they?* Shayma thought. *One wish down. Two to go.*

"NOW, LET ME THINK. I WANT TO WISH FOR SOMETHING REALLY GOOD. MAYBE A MANSION. TEN MANSIONS! FILLED WITH JEWELS!"

"No imagination." Mao-ming sighed. "Mortals always want the same things. Billions of dollars. Fancy yachts."

"Yadda yadda yadda," Inan agreed.

"I'd wish I could be light, like a sunbeam," said Ghul. The other four looked at him. "Just for a change," he said, blushing. "Not all the time."

"I'd wish for a cooler temper," Inan said.

"I'd wish to fly faster than I already do," said Nikolai, "if that's possible."

"I'd wish you two would stop fighting," said Mao-ming, "even for five minutes."

They all looked at Shayma. Waiting. She did not dare meet Nikolai's eyes.

Finally, Nikolai broke the silence. "I wish he'd make his last two wishes already, so we could get out of here," he said.

"I wish you'd shut up," said Inan.

"I wish I could think of something useful," Ghul said.

*Something useful.* Shayma wished *she* could be useful.

And then it came to her. "I know," she said. "I could offer to stay here in the bottle forever. If he'd let the rest of you go—"

"What?" cried Ghul. "Become a slave to that creature? Absolutely not!"

"It's not such a bad idea," Inan said.

Mao-ming glared at Inan.

"What I meant was, it's a terrible idea," Inan said.

"I wouldn't mind, honest," Shayma said in a small voice, even more frightened than she sounded.

"No!" said Ghul. "You can't just sacrifice yourself like that. I forbid it!" And the inside of the bottle went pitch-dark for several seconds. In the darkness, Ghul squeezed her hand, radiating warmth and affection.

Shayma squeezed his hand back. *I've been so blind*, she thought. *Just a blind little fool!*

"As I was saying. Now then," Ghul said, as the bottle lightened. "I wish I could think of something useful."

And Shayma got another idea. "I wish," she said, "I could grant you your wish."

For a moment no one dared to speak. The four younger djinn were all staring at Mao-ming.

"Is there a rule against it?" asked Nikolai. "Against one djinn granting another djinn's wishes?"

"Hmm," Mao-ming said. She was the best one at

memorizing the Vital Rules. "We can't use our powers for evil. We can't grant any of the Illegitimate Wishes." She nodded thoughtfully. "Yes, one wish each. I think that's allowed. But we've got to be careful, or we risk getting Cast Out."

That would be worse than a thousand years in a bottle.

"I wish" — Mao-ming began — "I wish that the mortal could hear me talking about the fabulous Treasure of Tabul."

"What good would that do?" said Nikolai, leaning forward to look at Mao-ming more closely. He grinned mischievously. "Oh, I get it. I grant your wish!"

Suddenly, Mao-ming's voice boomed. **"THE TREASURE OF TABUL MAKES ALL OTHER TREASURES PALE BY COMPARISON. THE MORTAL DOESN'T KNOW IT, BUT HE'D BE THE RICHEST BEING ON THE FACE OF THE EARTH IF HE COULD GET HIS HANDS ON THAT TREASURE."**

The other djinn began to smile, catching on.

The mortal was leaning so close to the bottle that his breath fogged the glass. "I HEARD THAT," he said. "WAIT."

His footsteps lumbered away. In a few minutes he was back.

"I JUST LOOKED IT UP ON THE INTERNET," he said. "THE TREASURE OF TABUL. SOME SAY IT'S BURIED IN THE DESERT. SOME SAY IT'S ONLY A MYTH. I DON'T INTEND TO WASTE MY SECOND WISH ON A FAIRY TALE."

The mortal was pacing around the room, chewing—it crunched like gravel but was probably just a bag of potato chips. *How long had it been since they'd eaten?* Shayma wondered.

"We had curry last night," Mao-ming reminded her, reading her thoughts again. "Mom cooked it as a special treat . . . for our good behavior."

"I love curry!" Ghul said.

Shayma's mother was a powerful djinn. The mere mention of her was enough to make Shayma lose her appetite.

"TELL YOU WHAT," said the mortal. "IF YOU TAKE ME TO THAT TREASURE OF TABUL WITHOUT USING ONE OF MY WISHES, I'LL LET YOU OUT EARLY. FOR GOOD BEHAVIOR."

**"DEFINE EARLY,"** Mao-ming said.

"EARLY IS SOONER RATHER THAN LATER," the mortal said.

**"YOU REALLY DON'T WANT THAT TREASURE. TRUST ME. IT'S TOO MUCH FOR ANY ONE MORTAL."**

"I'LL BE THE JUDGE OF THAT!" snapped the mortal. "TAKE ME TO IT."

**"THE LOCATION IS SECRET. DO YOU REALLY WANT TO GO THERE? AH, YOU SHOULDN'T! WITH ALL THAT WEALTH, IMAGINE HOW JEALOUS YOUR FRIENDS WOULD BE!"**

"YES, THEY WOULD BE, WOULDN'T THEY?" The mortal laughed. "GET ME AS CLOSE AS YOU CAN."

"May I try?" asked Ghul.

"Okay, Ghul," said Nikolai. "I wish you'd take us near the Treasure of Tabul."

They lurched and rolled, flung in all directions inside the bottle. When the upheaval finally stopped, Ghul was barely visible—he looked like a dark rain puddle at the bottom. *It must have used up all his powers*, Shayma thought, *to carry them so fast and so far*.

"WHERE AM I?" the mortal bellowed. "ALL I SEE IS A LAKE AND SOME STUPID TREES. TAKE ME TO THE TREASURE!"

Mao-ming asked, **"DO YOU WISH IT?"**

"YES!"

*Wish number two.*

They plunged below the lake. Shayma, with her keen sense of hearing, could detect the sound of bubbles whirling and popping all around them. She could almost feel the cold and dark of the water closing over them, and it made her tremble. She could barely dog-paddle. Ghul sloshed a little nearer to her.

*We'll all drown*, thought Shayma, bracing herself against the sides of the bottle. *All five of us and the mortal, too!*

"Don't worry, little sister," Mao-ming consoled her. "There's plenty of air for us here in the bottle."

Inan said, "I wish for an air bubble to protect the mortal. We mustn't get Cast Out for harming him!"

Mao-ming nodded and brought her thumb and forefinger together in a circle. "Wish granted," she said.

"THE BOTTOM OF A LAKE—WHAT AN IDIOTIC PLACE FOR A TREASURE!" the mortal roared as soon as he could utter a sound. "GET ME OUT OF HERE!"

**"DO YOU WISH IT?"** asked Mao-ming calmly.

"I WISH TO BE BACK HOME WITH THE TREASURE!" spluttered the mortal. "AND I WISH TO HEAVEN I'D NEVER LAID EYES ON ANY OF YOU DEVILISH DJINN!"

"How sad," said Mao-ming. "That we can grant him only *one* last wish."

"I wish him that very last wish," Shayma said

quickly, and Inan granted it. With a fizzing and a *pop!* the five djinn flew out into the night air. They landed, shivering, in a semicircle on the soft grass near the mortal's fountain, a few yards apart. Shayma bent her head and sniffed at the ground. The earth again! It smelled as rich and comforting as a cup of hot chocolate.

"Well done," Mao-ming said.

Now that the mortal had never laid eyes on them, Shayma thought, that meant he had never spotted them on his carpet in the light of day, or caught them, or stuffed them in a bottle, or forced them to grant three wishes. Best of all, her mother never needed to know a thing!

"I wish I could have seen his face when he got that last wish," Mao-ming grinned.

"I wish we could have one more ride on that carpet," Nikolai said dreamily.

"I wish you'd stop talking about flying carpets!" Inan sighed.

"I wish we were back home in time for dinner," Shayma said.

Ghul said, "I still have a wish left. Hmm . . . it's been a long time since I've eaten a really good curry."

And Shayma instantly granted this wish.

# Black Sheep of the Family

## by Patricia McCormick

It happened at the last Smith family reunion. Somewhere between the sack race and the egg toss. That's when I found out. That my parents weren't really my parents.

I'd always known there was something different about me—like that game on *Sesame Street* where the kids try to find the one thing on Maria's magic screen that doesn't belong there. Like I was a vowel and everybody else in my family was a consonant.

But it wasn't until my need for a sugar fix collided with my cousin Wally's need to practice for his learner's permit test that I understood why.

The rest of the extended family was in the backyard, playing goofy games. I'd just single-handedly lost the sack race for my branch of the Smith family tree and snuck off behind the garage to console myself with a bag of SuperPuff marshmallows I'd stolen from the s'mores supplies. Wally, who'd recently changed his name to Pierre and who was going through what my mom called "that rebellious stage," had just declared the egg toss an oppressive tribalistic ritual and walked off in protest—and was sitting in his parents' car in Gramma's driveway, practicing his driving without the motor running.

"What are you doing here?" he said when I opened the door and got in on the passenger side.

"That's what I'd like to know," I said, popping a SuperPuff in my mouth.

"What do you mean?" Wally/Pierre said, flicking on the imaginary turn signal.

"Wally, I'm the *only one* who can't do this stuff," I said.

"Pierre. The name's Pierre," he said, checking the rearview mirror.

"Pierre," I said. "I struck out in Wiffle ball. I dropped my water balloon on myself, and the only person I beat in the relay race was Grandpa. And that was after he gave me a head start."

"So?" Pierre made a ticking noise that was supposed to sound like the clicking of the turn signal.

"So what's the matter with me?" I licked the SuperPuff powder off my fingers and plucked another one out of the bag.

"Nothing." He glanced in the side-view mirror, then accelerated, stepping on the imaginary gas.

"So why can everyone else do this stuff but me?"

"Because . . ." he said. "You're adopted."

I chewed on my fifth SuperPuff marshmallow. If this had been a movie I would've started choking, and Pierre would've accidentally set the bag of marshmallows on fire when he knocked into the cigarette lighter while leaning across the seat to give me the Heimlich maneuver. Then the entire extended Smith family would have come running over with water balloons to put out the fire, and there would have been tears and hugs, and some goofy pet doing some goofy pet thing that would make everybody wipe away their tears before eating the roasted marshmallows. But I just kept chewing, and Pierre just kept driving.

What was weird was that I wasn't even that upset. What he said kind of made sense. I've always felt like I'm not really part of my family. They're all normal and calm. Boring, actually. I'm different: *Creative* is the word my mom uses for it. Emotional. Unpredictable. My parents are always telling me to simmer down, like I'm a pot of green beans. And my sisters are always calling me a freak. What they're basically saying is: Be like us. Don't be like whoever you are.

If I were adopted, it would explain a lot of things.

Besides, Pierre was fifteen. He was the oldest of all the cousins, had facial hair, and could drive like Will Ferrell in *Talladega Nights*. He had credibility.

"How come no one ever told me?" I said.

"I'm the only one who knows," he said. "And my parents. They said, 'Pierre, whatever you do, don't tell Jennifer.'"

"So why are you telling me?"

"Because it's time to break the cycle of oppression. Time to end the conspiracy."

Right about then, his mother called out for him from the other side of the garage. "Walllly!" she yelled. "Wally, it's time for hot dogs."

Pierre jumped out of the car without even putting it in park or turning off the imaginary engine. "Coming, *ma mère*," he hollered back, and disappeared. Leaving me with a runaway imaginary car—and a runaway imagination.

Since then, I have decided to gather evidence to determine the validity of Pierre's statement. I have also decided to treat it as a theory—and use the scientific method we learned last year in seventh grade to test it.

Here is what I have recorded so far in my science notebook under OBSERVATIONS.

### Ways I Am Not Like the Rest of My Family

1. I am 5 feet 9½ inches tall, wear size 11 shoes, and look like the letter *L* when I stand sideways. I'm still in middle school but almost as tall as my father and already taller than my mom and my twin sisters, Jill and Joan, who, even though they are two years older than me, are only 5 foot 7 and who look like the letter *P* from the side.

2. I am moody and morose and love tragic and meaningful books such as *The Catcher in the Rye* and *To Kill a Mockingbird*. My sisters are cheerful and sunny and can't even watch an episode of *Seventh Heaven* without a box of tissues at the ready.

3. I am not exactly a vegetarian because that would imply that I actually like vegetables. But I cannot stand the taste, smell, or idea of eating any kind of the 57 varieties of meat consumed on a regular basis by the members of my family. (My diet basically consists of pasta, pizza, and more pasta.)

4. Joan and Jill are the co-captains of the soccer team, basketball team, and volleyball team. I break out in a sweat just putting on my gym clothes.

5. I can, however, sing like a rock star. Jill and Joan

can shatter a windowpane with the first few notes of "Happy Birthday."

**Ways I Am Like the Rest of My Family**
1. We have the same last name.

There is more than just the unmistakable physical evidence that I do not belong in this family. As part of my quest, I get out the family photo albums. There are baby pictures of Jill and Joan in footie pajamas, looking like Thing 1 and Thing 2. There are pictures of them on their first birthdays, their first Christmas, and other assorted pictures documenting their adorable twinhood, with my mom in the background. (My dad is taking the photos.) Then there's the newborn picture of me, looking all pink and wrinkly. Then, the obligatory picture of Jill and Joan holding me and pretending they think I'm cute while secretly plotting to put me in the diaper pail. But in between, there are absolutely no pictures of my mom pregnant with me. None.

I decide to ask my mom about this. Slyly. Subtly. So she won't know exactly what I'm driving at. I wait until she comes home from her weekly exercise class.

"Have you lost weight, Mom?" I say.

She looks at herself in the mirror. "You think so?"

"Definitely," I say. "So, is it hard to get back in shape after you have a baby?"

She turns sideways, holds in her stomach, and surveys the result in the mirror. "Maybe I have lost a little," she says.

"I mean, did you go to exercise class after you had me?"

She is holding her breath, probably to see if this makes her look skinnier. Or perhaps she's stalling before she sits me down for the heart-to-heart chat she's been planning all these years. She exhales.

Now it's my turn to hold my breath.

"Honey," she says, "when you're running around after two-year-old twins and a newborn, you don't need an exercise class."

I feel vaguely disappointed by this answer because (1) it actually sort of makes sense, and (2) it doesn't really solve the mystery of whether or not I'm adopted. I decide to be more direct in my questioning.

"Come to think of it, Mom, there aren't any pictures of you pregnant with me."

She gives me a puzzled look. "There must be," she says. Then she bites her lower lip for a second like she's trying really hard to come up with an explanation. "Do you want to have chicken or pork chops tonight?" she says.

I make a note of two things: (1) that she changed the subject as soon as my questions got too probing, and (2) that a real mother would remember that her own daughter doesn't eat meat.

That night I go online and visit a site called Gene Scene, which uses genetic testing to help people figure out if their kids are really their kids or, in my case, if their parents are really their parents. Gene Scene seems mainly to be used by women who are trying to get their boyfriends to pay child support, boyfriends who are trying to get out of paying child support, and wannabe heiresses. But they do offer a couple of DNA test kits that sound promising. The first one involves getting blood samples from all the parties involved. This, obviously, will not work because there is no casual way for me to ask my parents if we all can spend a little quality time at the doctor's office getting our blood drawn.

Then there's what Gene Scene calls the Discreet Test. All you have to do is collect a DNA sample from the person or people you want to test and mail it to the Gene Scene lab. I get out my notebook and make a list of what I'll need for the discreet test.

## Materials

1. DNA specimens, e.g., sweaty T-shirts, fingernail clippings, socks, licked stamps, chewed gum, used dental floss, used tissue
2. Plastic bag for collecting the specimens and mailing them to Gene Scene
3. $695

The Discreet Test is obviously too disgusting—I nearly break out in hives at the idea of collecting used dental floss from the trash can in my parents' bathroom—and too expensive. So I click on the box that says FREE DNA TEST.

Gene Scene explains, in complicated scientific language involving terms such as dominant and recessive genes, that you can use eye color to determine if your parents are your parents. There is even a box where you can enter the eye color of the mother, father, and child, and Gene Scene will automatically tell you if the father is a likely match. I enter my mom's eye color: hazel. Mine: dark brown. And my father's: green. Then I click on SUBMIT. One second later, a message pops up on my screen. The alleged father is "likely excluded" from being the biological father.

I get a rotten feeling in my stomach. Not just because the computer has just referred to my dad as the "alleged father," which makes him sound like some kind of criminal, but because what Wally/Pierre said may actually be true.

Like any good detective, I decide to go and verify the precise color eyes Joan and Jill have. The people I have always thought of as my sisters are in the den watching TV with the person I have always thought of as my mom. A commercial comes on, and they start laughing. My mom turns to Jill and says, "I knew you'd say that!" I interrupt this warm, fuzzy, mother-daughter bonding scene to ask Jill what color her eyes are. They all stop laughing and stare at me. "Why do you care?" Jill says.

"Because I think there's something different about me," I say.

"There is," says Joan. "You're a freak."

The commercial is over. My mom turns back to the screen. "Honestly, Jen, sometimes you say the funniest things."

I go back to my notebook. The scientific method says you are supposed to come up with a hypothesis based on your observations. Here is what I write.

## Hypothesis
I am the real child of a famous couple—creative, unpredictable, and emotional people who gave me away to a nice, ordinary family named the Smiths to

shield me from the harsh light of publicity, the paparazzi, and the high-powered Beverly Hills lifestyle until they could come get me. It's like the Angelina Jolie–Brad Pitt adoptions in reverse, a witness-protection plan for the kids of the rich and famous.

I add supporting data to my notebook.

## Other Examples of Famous Offspring Raised by Ordinary Adoptive Parents

1. Luke Skywalker
2. The Ugly Duckling

Then I make a list of my potential famous parents.

## Possible Long-Lost Famous Parents

1. J. D. Salinger and Harper Lee. A logical choice, because they are the authors of my two favorite books. But I go online and see that they are technically way too old to have had me and that they live in different parts of the country.
2. Hugh Grant and Uma Thurman. Possible, because I have long legs like Uma and floppy hair like Hugh. This theory, however, does not hold up because if they were my parents I'd be a lot better-looking.
3. Bruce Springsteen and Lucinda Williams. All signs point to Bruce and Lucinda. I have long legs,

a flat chest, wild hair, and can sing like a banshee. I investigate this possibility further by going on-line where I hit the celebrity parent theory jack-pot: Bruce and Lucinda were both at the Grammy Awards in 1993, the year of my conception.

All experiments are supposed to have a control group, so I also write down information about Todd and Becky Smith, the people I have, up until now, thought of as my actual parents.

### Witness Protection Program Parents

1. Todd Smith. Todd is a podiatrist who treats old ladies with bunions and collects stamps for a hobby. He cuts the lawn every weekend, takes out the recycling on Tuesdays, and plays golf on Sundays.
2. Becky Smith. Becky is the receptionist at Todd's office and makes needlepoint Christmas ornaments all year long as a hobby. She vacuums the house every weekend, makes meat loaf on Tuesdays, and teaches Sunday school every Sunday.

For the next few days, I occupy myself with images of my moving reunion with Bruce and Lucinda. It's an emotional moment—Bruce and Lucinda beg my forgiveness and hope I understand that they did the whole witness protection thing for my own good.

Todd and Becky are heartbroken, but they know they have to let me go for the good of my career as a rock star. Jill and Joan are green with jealousy, but I'm magnanimous about the whole thing. I don't tell Bruce and Lucinda about how Jill and Joan called me a freak, and I even let Jill and Joan ask my new-found parents for autographs. Bruce and Lucinda and I climb on the tour bus, laughing about how we all just happen to be wearing the same Levi's jean jacket. We turn and wave good-bye to Todd and Becky and Jill and Joan in their matching L.L. Bean fleece zip-ups.

During this period, I also consider having a heart-to-heart with Todd and Becky, as I now think of them, telling them it's okay, that I know the truth. I plan on telling them they've done the best they could and that it's probably better for us all if they send me back to my real parents now. I'll comfort them. I'll give Todd a little squeeze on the shoulder, the way he always did when I was cut from the soccer team, the basketball team, or the volleyball team. Becky will frown the way she does when she's worried, so that it looks like there are parentheses on either side of her mouth. They'll ask how I figured it out. I'll tell them about Gene Scene. Jill and Joan will help me pack. And I'll send them all really expensive Christmas gifts when I'm touring with Bruce and

Lucinda. (Although it's possible I'll just give Jill and Joan leftovers from the goodie bags we get at various charity balls.)

I feel a little bad having these thoughts—like I'm the one with the secret, like I'm the one hiding something from them. Even though they're the ones who've been keeping my true identity from me.

Meanwhile, I do the Gene Scene eye test, plugging in Bruce and Lucinda's eye color. It's a match.

Which makes me feel surprisingly bad. I know a scientific researcher is supposed to be unbiased. But I have to confess: Ever since that day eating Super-Puffs behind the garage with Wally, I haven't been able to stop wishing that my parents weren't really my parents. Now that it looks like that really might be true, I wish it weren't.

I take a deep breath and decide to go downstairs to face the moment of truth with Todd and Becky. They're sitting in the den. Todd has his bifocals on the tip of his nose as he looks over his stamp book. Becky has a needlepoint Santa in her lap.

Todd looks up at me. "What's the matter, Jen?"

I shrug.

"You've got that same frown on your face, just like your mother's."

I duck into the powder room and look in the mirror. It's true. There are two curved lines around my mouth—not parentheses exactly, but at least commas.

I come back out to the den.

"Is it true?" I say. "What Pierre said?"

"Who's Pierre?" Todd says.

"He used to be Wally," says Becky.

I take a deep breath. "Pierre says I'm adopted."

Todd and Becky exchange a glance, using that silent parental code of communication to decide who's going to go first. Becky puts her Santa down. Todd pushes his glasses up to the bridge of his nose.

"Jen, honey . . ." Becky says. She doesn't seem to know how to finish.

"Why would you think that?" says Todd. Clearly, he's stalling for time.

"Because," I say, "I'm not like the rest of you."

They just look at each other. At least they don't lie.

"Pierre says it's because I'm adopted. He says he's the only one who knows and that his parents made him promise not to tell."

Becky sighs. "Pierre also says that Twinkies have traces of rat poison in them and that Osama bin Laden is living in Maplewood, New Jersey."

Good points, even I have to admit. "Then why am I so tall? Why am I such a klutz? How come I'm such a good singer? Why am I so moody and creative and unpredictable?"

Todd smiles. "Because you're *you*."

"So I'm not adopted?"

My mom smiles. "You're one of a kind, Jen," she says. "But you're *our* kind."

"Why aren't there any pictures of you pregnant with me?"

"The truth?" says my dad. "I was still in medical school, and we already had your sisters. We were barely scraping by. Your grandma Smith sent us money for a family portrait—you know, the kind they do at a photography studio. But your mom insisted we use the money for a crib for you."

"Really?" I say.

"Really," they both say.

This is turning into an emotionally moving moment after all, even without Bruce and Lucinda. Being emotional, I am about to cry. I notice, too, that my normal, calm father is also about to cry. He takes off his bifocals and comes over and gives my shoulder a little squeeze.

I'm close to solving this case, and decide it's time to confront the perp—in other words, to double-check the color of my dad's eyes. "What color are your eyes?" I ask him.

"I don't know," he says. "Hazel, I guess. Sometimes they look green. Why?"

I know then, without even checking with the people at Gene Scene, that these nice, normal people are my parents. My secretly emotional father, and my mother with a frown like parentheses. I also know, thanks to Gene Scene, that there's nothing wrong with being a black sheep. Most sheep are white because that's the dominant gene; only a few have the gene for black wool. The special ones. The unpredictable ones.

# The Fashion Contest

**by Catherine Stine**

"Today you'll pick a partner for your colonial history project," says our teacher, Mr. Thompson. The classroom buzzes as we look around for prospects. Mr. Thompson shushes us. "I'm going to ask kids in alphabetical order. Joanna Atwater."

That's me. I'm the only kid whose name starts with *A*. "Um . . ." I point to my best soccer bud, Jake, but Jake's smiling at his other friend, Mac. The boys all want me on their soccer team because I score goals. But for projects, boys don't usually pick girls. It's only cool to admit liking a girl on a T3 list, but more about that soon.

Mr. Thompson says, "Nice to see you try a new partner, Jo." What's he talking about? Jake isn't a new partner. "Candace and you will be an interesting duo."

Huh? My finger must have been wavering in Candace's direction when I saw Jake smile at Mac. She sits two seats away from Jake. During recess Candace acts stupid. She clicks photos of the boys with her cell phone. Her friends gather around her, screeching like hyenas on caffeine. Me? I play soccer during recess.

"But that's not who I pointed to," I blurt. "I, uh . . ."

Mr. Thompson peers at me with an it's-incredibly-rude-to-admit-you-don't-want-to-work-with-someone expression. So I'm stuck with Candace—the too-giggly girlie-girl who's numero uno on Gavin, my crush's, T3 list. Gavin's the captain of the soccer team.

Okay, what's a T3 list? It's like a top ten list, but with just a top three. The girls write their top three crushes, and so do the guys. Then when Mr. Thompson turns to write on the board, kids fold the T3s into tiny squares and toss them. The room fills with T3 confetti. And it's a grab-fest! Mine's always:

1. Gavin—best soccer captain
2. Spud—lanky lead singer of the Potatoheads
3. Jake—best soccer defense dude

Jake's only on my list because he's my best friend, so if I don't include him he'll be hurt. We always include each other last as a courtesy.

My big secret wish is to be number one on Gavin's list or have him gaze at me with his green leprechaun eyes. If he did, I wouldn't screech like Candace and her friends do. I'd simply smile back coolly even though I'd be whooping inside.

People say I'm cute enough with my shaggy blond hair, long legs, and friendly smile. But whenever I intercept Gavin's T3, it's always the same:

1. Candace—super hottie
2. Iris—IM goddess
3. Gwyneth—lead singer for the Mermaidens

I'm never on it. Oh, as you might've figured, everyone picks at least one famous band member. It's a safe yet trendy choice. *Any-hoo*, while the rest of my classmates pick partners, I sit in shock about having to work on a history project with Candace.

Mr. Thompson says, "Now, kids. Move next to your new partner to discuss project ideas—something inventive that shows an aspect of the Colonial period we've been studying, from around 1750 to 1775."

From across the room, Candace eyeballs me warily, as if my being the only girl on the soccer team is a contagious plague. Hey, I'm eyeing her suspiciously, too. Is the obsession with donning leotards under frilly minis and wearing pink slippers even though you're hardly a ballet dancer contagious?

She's not budging. So reluctantly, I get up, shuffle across the room, and pull up a chair next to Ms. Pretentious-Cell-Phone-Photog. "Hi," I mutter.

Candace's mouth puckers up like a catfish. "I'm in charge, Joanna," she declares.

She dares say this to the best goal-scorer? "Like heck you are."

"I'm good at fashion and dancing," she announces, ignoring my comment, "so it's either colonial fashion or a dance project."

Hoop skirts? Argh! Learning colonial dance steps would be torture, plus we'd have to dance with each other. "Neither," I say firmly.

"Any other bright ideas?" she asks, arching an eyebrow.

"Let's build an Indian village," I suggest. I love the idea of carving longboats from corkboard and making tepees from paper rolled into cones.

"Too hard. Way too many elements."

"I've got a good one! Colonial sports."

"You *would* think of that." She's openly scowling now. "I don't *play* sports."

I scowl back. "That's why I picked Jake."

"Well, Jake picked Mac." Candace taps her pink glossy fingernails on the top of her desk, which drives any other good project possibility out of my head.

"Class, almost done?" asks Mr. Thompson. Everyone groans. "Five more minutes," he says, pacing around the room.

Candace beams. "Guess we'll have to go with one of my suggestions."

I'm not dancing with her. My heart goes *tim, tim,* like my mom's needle against her metal thimble. That's when I think of my sewing machine. It's the one girlie activity I actually find cool. I even took lessons at the Y last year and made a shirt. After having to rip out the sleeves twice because of puckers, I finally mastered the art of cutting teensy slits in the fabric to ease the sleeve around the sleeve holes. "Do you sew?" I ask her.

Candace looks doubtful. "A little. I made a doll pillowcase once."

I nod. She has no clue how much harder it would be to make an entire colonial dress. "Okay," I say, "let's do fashion."

Candace almost smiles at me, but then the corners of her mouth turn down.

We go over to the bookshelf and pull out illustrated books on the 1700s. I read some fashion terms out loud. "'*Echelle*—a ladderlike decoration of braid, ribbons, and bows across the neckline. *Polonaise*—a dress with a close-fitting waist and full skirt looped to form three panels and festoons.'" Sounds hard, even for me.

"What are festoons?" asks Candace.

"Who knows?" I hand her the book, and she pores over it.

Next we look at Native American clothes. Cute fringe boots, feathers bursting out of a lady's headband. I love the fact that Indians knew how to get around in the forest and respected nature so much. Candace frowns. "Ew! It's all yucky animal skins and dirty feathers from the woods."

"Suits me fine," I say. "You do colonial dames, and I'll do Native Americans."

"Deal!" Her big brown eyes light up. I picture her brain already selecting prissy crinoline and satin from the fabric store. Candace narrows her eyes. "But Indian outfits are easier than colonial dresses, right?" she asks.

"Maybe." My mood sinks. Then I realize that even a simple Indian dress would baffle Candace. Either way I will outsew her. "Okay, whatever. You do the Native American fashion," I say. I drag my sneaker over the linoleum floor. It makes a nice annoying squeak.

Candace screws up her freckled nose. "I changed my mind again. I hate all that stinky leather. I'll stick with the colonial outfits."

"You'll do fine," I lie, thinking that she wouldn't have had to use real deer hide because there's plenty of fake leather around.

Candace bounces her chestnut-colored hair on her shoulders. "Yeah. I'll do great. I'll even challenge you to a history fashion walk-off."

"What's that?" I pull at my scruffy bangs and sneak a peek at Gavin. He's running a hand through his amazingly red hair as he laughs with his friend Carlos.

"Pay attention, Joanna." Candace jiggles my arm. "It's when we take turns walking down the runway," she explains. "It's a fashion competition." She giggles like crazy, probably picturing me tripping down the runway in floppy moccasins.

Modeling isn't my favorite idea, but she's bound to lose. "You're on, but no help from your friends or mom."

"No danger of that," she says. We shake on it. Her hand feels clammy.

We announce our plans to Mr. Thompson. "Intriguing," he says.

That weekend Mom drives me to the mall. At the craft shop I buy beads, pearly shells, and acrylic paint.

At the fabric store I choose faux leather and thread. From the Halloween store, I buy face paint and my best find, a jumbo bag of dyed turkey feathers.

By sending e-mails back and forth (easier than arguing in person), Candace and I finally agree to each make three outfits.

On Monday, when I walk into school, I see posters in the halls. They say:

**HISTORY FASHION WALK-OFF: COME ONE, COME ALL!**
**MONDAY, OCTOBER 24TH AT 2 P.M.**
**IN MR. THOMPSON'S 6TH-GRADE CLASS**
**CANDACE THE COLONIAL DAME**
**VS. JOANNA THE NATIVE AMERICAN**

Waves of fury crash through me. Candace has certainly been busy making obnoxious promotional materials.

That afternoon when I walk into class, two kids say, "Go, Joanna." Then, when Candace bounces in, lots of kids shout, "Yay, Candace!" The walk-off isn't until next Monday, but the popularity contest has already begun. Mr. Thompson tells everyone to be quiet and get out our books. I've underestimated Candace. My competitive juices sizzle, like when our soccer team's about to play our toughest rivals. I'll need cheerleaders.

At practice, I ask Jake to cheer for me. "But fashion's dumb, Jo," he says.

"I know," I say, "but I bet your project seems silly, too." He agrees.

None of the guys on my soccer team are willing to make any promises. And I don't have the nerve to ask Gavin, because he's busy coaching. I'm actually scared to talk to him. Instead, I simply admire how his fiery hair flies back when he runs.

By the end of Wednesday afternoon, the only kids who've promised to cheer for me are Simon, my lab partner, who's always blowing his nose, and Thelma, a new girl who moved here to Pennsylvania from Arkansas. She doesn't fit into any clique.

I'm getting worried.

Fortunately, designing and getting ready to sew makes me feel better. That night, on the floor in my room, I cut pieces for an ankle-length prairie dress. I paint zigzag patterns across each piece. Then I fringe the borders with scissors. When I sew the sections together and turn the dress right side out, I gasp. It's absolutely amazing! I IM Jake.

Me: How's your history project going?

Jake: Mac and I R doing wacky facts. But he's lazy. I'm doing all the work. Wish I had U as my partner!!!!!

Me: Now U tell me! Name a wacky fact.

Jake: The first flush toilet was invented in the 1770s.

Me: ☺ FUNNEEEE!!!!! What are Gavin and Carlos doing?

Jake: Why R U always asking about Gavin? They're doing a fake Declaration of Independence scroll. Bo-rrring & UN-original.

If Jake weren't my best friend, I'd detect a hint of jealousy between him and Gavin. Too weird.

Thursday at recess, before we play soccer, I see Candace talking to Jake. She's standing close to him, and he doesn't back off like he usually does with girls other than me. Gavin glances over at them, too. His smile gets lopsided, then fades. The whole thing makes me cringe. What's Candace up to now?

That afternoon in history class, as Mr. Thompson turns to the board to write a list of early settlers such as the Dutch and the Swedes, kids toss a snowstorm of white T3s into the air. I catch Gavin's.

1. Candace—super-hot colonial model
2. Iris—IM goddess
3. Gwyneth—lead singer for the Mermaidens

I look at Gavin and sigh as Mr. Thompson reels off more names of settlers. Such sea-green eyes! He gazes at Candace. Just once could he look at me like that?

But what really gets under my skin has nothing to do with Gavin. It has to do with what I read on Jake's T3 list that someone's just passed me.

1. Candace—cute colonial dame
2. Lilu—singer from the Lollipops
3. Joanna—best soccer offense

Jake put Candace first? He's never, ever done that before! It must be because she's been talking to him, probably conning him into cheering for her. He'll never go for that . . . will he? Jake's *my* buddy.

Payback time.

After class, I take a deep breath, straighten my shoulders, and walk up to Gavin. He's stuffing his binder in his pack. I ask if he'll cheer for me at the walk-off. Still looking down he says, "If you're better. May the best person win." That's good enough for me!

Candace has seen me talking to Gavin. I can tell she's worried, because her thin eyebrows are curved down. I walk with a sly grin out of the classroom.

Just as I'm getting my shin guards out of my locker, she prances over. "Hey, Joanna," she says. "How are the Indian costumes coming along?"

"Fine," I say, and ask about hers.

"I'm working on something guaranteed to have kids cheer for me," she replies. Her crafty brown eyes gleam. "Including Jake."

"So?" I say as boldly as I can. "I've got Gavin's vote."

"No way. You're too much of a tomboy." She laughs and minces away.

This is getting too spiteful for words. I'm shaking, I'm so mad.

Again, the only thing that makes me feel better is the actual sewing—that, and picturing Candace stitching a dress inside out. It's Friday night and I'm crafting leggings out of fake orange leather. The walk-off is this Monday—only two more days. So far I've made a beaded shirt and a prairie dress. Mom treated me to a pair of real mocs. My shaggy hair is too short to braid, but when I try stuff on I look like a fairly convincing Delaware Indian. I've also made two Native American sports items. The boys in my class should like that. Or is sports fashion too tomboyish?

On Saturday I leap out of bed, head to the kitchen, and gobble down cereal. I'm eager to finish my project.

"How's it going?" asks my mom. She's made many a great garment in her day.

"Okay. Today I'm making my best costume."

"Oh? What?" She puts down her coffee mug and leans forward in her chair.

I feel a flutter of happiness. "An Indian princess dress with a cape made from turkey feathers."

"That sounds beautiful," she answers. "Need any help?"

"We're not supposed to get sewing help. Just to have you around is kind of helpful." I smile. "You know, moral support."

"Any time." She kisses me on my forehead.

I go upstairs to cut out the wide cape. I sew in layers of feathers—green, blue, red, golden. I try it on. Whoa! I look like a Native American movie star. Even if Gavin thinks I'm a hopeless tomboy, he'll change his mind when he sees me in this.

The phone rings. I let Mom get it; it's usually for her. Mostly I just get e-mails about soccer games. Mom calls me from downstairs. I run to open my door. "What?" I shout. She yells back that it's for me.

My heart patters. Who could it be? Is it Gavin on the other line, waiting to say he'll cheer for me on Monday? Probably not. Maybe it's Jake telling me he's got my back. Either would be a big relief. I pick up the phone. "Hullo?"

Mom clicks off. "Hi, Jo." It's Candace. She sounds upset. She's never called me Jo before.

"What's up?" I ask, concerned despite my misgivings.

"I need you to come over. *Right now.*"

Controlling Candace is back. "I'm busy," I answer coldly.

"But you have to come over. I'm having . . . a fashion emergency."

I think, *no kidding!* But she sounds desperate. So I agree.

I bike over to her house and ring the bell. Even though she lives in the same neighborhood, I've never been here. Her house is grander than mine, with a manicured lawn that has an actual burbling fountain.

Candace opens the door. It's dark inside, though it's only afternoon. Her eyes are puffy and her normally shiny hair is greasy. It's pulled back into a ponytail, which shocks me. "C'mon in," she says, swinging the door shut behind me. A poodle with a polka-dot bow on its head races over. It growls like it wants to sink its teeth in my leg. "Off, Chanel!" says Candace. The dog pays no attention.

"Is your mom or dad here?" I ask as we climb up the darkened staircase with Chanel nipping at my heels.

"No. My mother works on the weekend." No mention of her dad. Maybe he doesn't live here.

"What does your mom do?" I ask boldly while turning to shoo away Chanel.

"She's an actress." Candace says proudly, with a hint of something else under it. Thankfully, she closes her bedroom door and leaves Chanel hyperventilating in the hall.

Candace's room is mind-boggling. She's got a giant TV, a computer with a broad, flat monitor, a canopied bed, and wall-to-wall white carpeting. It reminds me of an ad for a penthouse suite in a four-star hotel. She points to her desk. On it is a mountain of wrinkled satin and lace. Clearly, she spent a fortune at the fabric store.

"You'll help sew my last outfit," she announces. What makes Candace think she can go around announcing what other people are going to do?

Her mess is not my problem. But I go over, anyway, and untangle the dress, try to lay it out flat. It could be pretty, except that the sleeves are puckered, the ribbon bodice is crooked, and the petticoat's uneven. Plus, it's *way* too loosely sewn by hand. "Don't you have a sewing machine?" I ask, incredulous.

She waves her hand as if batting off a dumb idea. "Nah. Sew it by hand."

"But I'm still working on mine. I mean, that wasn't part of our deal."

"We're partners." Candace glares at me. "You *have* to help me."

"Then call off that stupid fashion walk-off," I say, placing a hand on my hip and glaring back at her. "Putting up posters wasn't part of the deal, either."

"It's just to build up enthusiasm. We have to go through with it now."

"Why?"

"Because it's part of the project. And Mr. Thompson's expecting it."

"I don't think he cares about that part."

"You're wrong. Besides, if you don't help, I'll tell on you." Her eyes practically spit fire.

I stand there with my mouth hanging open. Who taught her to talk to people like that? All right, if she wants me to sew a seam, I will. Sort of. But no major handiwork.

An hour later, when I climb back down that creepy spiral staircase, her mom still isn't home. Even Chanel looks forlorn as she follows me, her tongue wagging between pointy teeth. Candace might have a warm glow from those oversized monitors in her room, but the rest of the house is darkly foreboding.

\* \* \*

Finally, it's Monday, history class. My costumes are ready to go, protected under plastic that Mom got me from the cleaners. Candace has set up a dressing room with folding screens the art teacher lent us. The runway will be the central space between the desks.

I hardly listen to most of the presentations because my heart is racing. Jake and Mac's is the first one funny enough to focus on—especially when Jake clicks his teeth and says, "The first porcelain false teeth were invented in the 1770s."

And Mac says, "Back then, there was a wild craze for rhubarb." Who would've known? We mostly just hear about Indians sharing their corn and beans.

Of course I perk up for Gavin's presentation. He and Carlos unroll a crinkled scroll. It's supposed to be the Declaration of Independence. Their calligraphy is okay, even though it veers uphill and has fat blots where the pen leaked. And there are misspellings, most notably, "Ben Funklin."

Mr. Thompson points out more misspellings but says, "Well done, boys."

Carlos and Gavin slink back to their seats. Still no cute wink from Gavin!

"Joanna and Candace, you're up next," says Mr. Thompson. The class starts to whoop as if they've been waiting for our presentation to let it rip.

"Walk-off!" they shout. My nerves jangle. My legs are rubber. But I manage to get out of my seat, go behind the screen, and struggle into my costume.

I go first, modeling the prairie dress. "Delaware Indians used shells, beads, and paint to decorate their clothes," I say. It's odd to walk past Gavin and think that he's checking me out. I peek over at him. Maybe I'll get my wish, and he'll be gazing back dreamily. But no, he turns away. My motley cheering section, Simon and Thelma, attempt some shy whoops. Then Jake calls, "Go, Jo!" and I feel a little better.

Candace is up next. I watch from behind the screen as she prances down the aisle in a nightgown. The boys whistle. Mr. Thompson glares at them.

"Colonial ladies wore a dormouse to sleep," Candace says, pointing to her pouffy hat, which looks like it's from a Halloween store. Plus, she's wearing her own pj's. *Cheater,* I think, fuming.

My turn. I tromp out, wearing my cool leather-fringe breeches. In one hand is my handmade lacrosse racket, in the other is a fake-hide football stuffed with leaves. "The Indians introduced lacrosse to the settlers," I say. "They also played a version of football—men and women together—with no tackling." This time my cheerleaders cheer loudly, and a chorus of boys join in. I was right about the sports equipment. Hands down, Jo wins this round, I say to myself. But on my way back, I still can't catch Gavin's eye. "Just wait until I emerge in my wondrous feather cape. Just wait until I'm the Indian princess," I chant under my breath. "Gavin will be under my spell. Jake, too."

Next, Candace walks the runway in her awful satin dress. "Colonial dames wore fancy dresses. This is called the echelle," she says, pointing to the crooked ribbons. When she lifts her arm, all the ugly puckers under the sleeves show. Gavin gasps and snickers. He laughs loudly. How rude! Candace's girlfriends scowl at Gavin. They attempt a halfhearted cheer, and one of them even takes a cell photo of Candace when Mr. Thompson's not looking. But Candace struggles in the lopsided dress. Thelma starts to get the giggles; Simon, too. I feel sweet revenge, but mixed with something else—pity?

"Kids, be civil," Mr. Thompson warns.

Candace takes one more step, trips on a droopy section of petticoat, and stumbles. I hear a *rrrrip*. Her skirt falls to the floor! Her pink slip is showing. The boys hoot. Only Jake is quiet, clapping a hand over his mouth. Candace grabs her skirt and runs back behind the screens. She looks at me.

Her face tells a story—a story of a tiny girl with sad brown eyes, needing attention.

"I feel bad for you, Candace," I say quietly. An idea comes to me. I suddenly want to help her for real. I whisper my plan. She nods, smiles. The first warm smile she's ever offered me. Quickly, we change. The class shuffles impatiently in their seats. "Walk-off! Walk-off!" kids chant, before Mr. Thompson again quiets them down.

I appear first from behind the screen, wearing my Indian princess dress. But instead of my feather cape, I have on Candace's lace cape. There are big gaps in the lace that dangle. A few kids attempt a whoop. I look at Jake. He screws up his face in confusion, then shouts, "Go, Jo!"

"After a time of getting used to each other," I say, "the Native Americans adopted some colonial customs, including the settlers' use of cotton and wool, which dry more quickly than deer hide." I finger the badly sewn cape as an example.

Jake cheers again. Other kids join in. Gavin wears his lopsided grin.

Next, Candace comes out. Everyone goes bonkers. Of course they do! I've given her my precious feather cape to wear. It's hard seeing it on her, but oddly satisfying, too. She twirls around to show it off and then waits for kids to quiet down. "The Indians also influenced the settlers. Colonial men adopted leather breeches for hunting, and colonial dames copied the pretty feathered and beaded decorations of the Native American women." She twirls once more, setting off another round of wild cheers.

"I guess you won the walk-off," I say to Candace afterward.

"They cheered for *your* amazing cape." Her eyes sparkle. "I told all my friends you made it, and they were like, wow! So let's call it a tie." I nod. That sounds fair.

At lunch, Jake says he admires me for letting Candace wear the cape.

"Thanks. It was tough," I admit. My face goes hot at what I want to say next. "Gavin was so rude. I couldn't believe he was laughing at Candace, the girl he supposedly likes. Jake, I admire you for not laughing at her, too."

It's Jake's turn to blush.

Later, at soccer practice, Gavin's apparently heard about the cape from Candace. Everyone has. He comes right up to me and says, "You're super creative." I beam. He adds, "You could design all kinds of stuff." He looks at me, really looks.

"Really?" I say. "I think so, too." Gavin has officially gazed at me with his emerald eyes, so I got my secret wish. But what's weirder than weird is that even before he does, I've already realized it's no longer my wish!

The next day during history, the T3s go flying. Mr. Thompson wheels around while they're in mid-flight. I can't believe it's taken him this long to catch us in the act. "No more of this!" he shouts, and takes them all.

Funny, I'm not even curious about what Gavin wrote. It has nothing to do with me being a tomboy, or not passing any popularity contest, or making a new friend in Candace. It has something to do with my new T3 list—the one that's now in Mr. Thompson's trash can. Because, for once, Jake is first.

Plus, I got a dream come true that I didn't even wish for.

I am designing a new logo and uniforms for our entire soccer team!

# The Reason I Will Love John MacFarlane Jr. Until the Day I Die

**by Rachel Vail**

Lather, rinse, repeat. An endless loop. I stood under the hot, pounding water and let the shampoo stream over my face, over my closed eyes, and tried not to think. Or to think only about shampoo. Shampoo, shampoo, shampoo. If you say anything enough times in a row, it sounds like gibberish, but shampoo is in a class by itself.

Ugh.

Everything brings me back to my brother and what he is going to face this morning, heading into school for the first time in two months. To class, by himself.

*It would be better if it were me*, I thought again, for the billionth time. Poor Calvin; it's not fair. He already has so much to deal with. Life bumps hard up against Calvin. I used to think maybe he was bringing it on himself; if he would just toss the ball back instead of getting all weird and possessive and wanting to pretend it's a pizza . . . if he would just act normal, he'd have friends, he'd get chosen in gym, he'd have people to sit with at lunch. But maybe he didn't choose all that weird awkwardness any more than he chose cancer.

I blinked my stinging eyes but didn't let myself rub them, and I grabbed the conditioner. It was still way early—I had gotten out of bed in the deep gray before six—so I rubbed the conditioner into my hair, from roots to ends, and then shaved my legs, even though I had already done them yesterday. Maybe I'd wear shorts to school. It was hot already, really hot for May.

My mother had bought me two new T-shirts. Maybe I'd wear one of them, so Calvin wouldn't be the only one wearing new clothes. He'd lost so much weight that none of his old worn-in clothes fit, and my mother had already given all his old stuff away to the Salvation Army. Calvin doesn't like new clothes. My mother washed everything four times for him and cut out all the tags. Man, even when he was little, Calvin would jump like he was scalded if a tag touched his skin.

I had to smile, thinking of how he looked back then, a study in circles—big chubby red cheeks, huge round brown eyes, loopy blond curls. So different from now.

Nicked my leg. Ouch. The blood ran down my shin, split into capillaries across the tub bottom, dripped patiently down the drain.

I rinsed the conditioner from my hair.

I shouldn't have said anything to Mackey. It's not that I thought he would make fun of Calvin. No way. The opposite, if anything. But—no. It's just that, well, we're pretty private in my family. Was I asking for sympathy? How unfair is that? Or attention? What Calvin had whispered to me just tore a hunk out of my heart, and I'm not even sure why.

"I wish for once I could just blend in," he'd said, without looking up from the computer game he was playing in the den. I wasn't sure, at first, if he was talking to me or to himself.

"You wish what?" I asked him. I was chugging orange juice from a tall glass, still sweating after soccer practice.

"Stupid, huh?" he said. "Waste a wish on that. Should wish for a cure, for remission."

"Yeah," I said. "How you feeling today?"

"But still I wish it," Calvin said, then grunted. A crash and an explosion lit the screen. "I died," he explained, and turned off the game.

I drained my glass.

He swiveled in his chair. "Not that I blended in before, but now, well, Monday morning, I'm not just the weird kid walking into school all alone, but the weird, sick, bald kid with a terminal disease."

I forced a smile. "You look good bald."

"Yeah?"

"Nobody will even notice."

He blinked slowly, his no-eyelash eyes closing and opening in their weirdly birdlike way. "Sure. Lots of kids in middle school are bald."

I didn't know what to say, so I just put my hand on his bony shoulder for a few seconds.

"Want to play Doom with me?" he asked.

I *so* didn't. "I have to take a shower."

I went up to my room. That night, when I went to a party one of the guys was having, Mackey and I took a walk, and I told him what Calvin had said. He put his arm around me, and we just walked along the deserted streets in the dark together. It felt good but also bad. We've been going out almost a year, me and Mackey, and have been friends even longer than that. It's not like with a lot of kids in eighth grade—getting from *will you go out with me?* to *we have to talk*, as fast as possible. There's no drama with us. Nowhere on my notebooks does it say Mrs. Jodie MacFarlane, Mr. and Mrs. John MacFarlane Jr., or even just Jodie and Mackey. He did write our initials like an addition problem on the back of his math notebook. But then, he's a nut.

We're more like best friends, which is a little weird for me because I've never really had a best friend before, just mostly teammates. Mackey and I crack each other up, and shoot hoops, and study for tests together, and a couple of times he talked about his father, who died a few years ago. When Calvin was diagnosed, Mackey said, "Oh, Jodie," and pulled me into a bear hug so tight I thought I might suffocate in there. Maybe I hoped I would.

I am not the girlfriend type. I am more of a sweaty-gym-socks, laugh-at-fart-jokes girl. Still, the fact is, I have a boyfriend. I have someone to talk to, someone to vent to about my brother and how much it hurt me to think about how much it was going to hurt him to walk into school Monday morning. That's what felt good, and also what felt bad.

Who does Calvin have?

I looked in the mirror as I dried off. *Okay*, I

thought. *I guess that's who.* I combed out my hair, toweled it roughly dry, and pulled it back in a pony-tail. *He's got me.*

Hard to say if that would help at all.

I'm a grade ahead of him, nineteen months older, a girl. What he really needed this morning was a gang of buddies, pals to walk into school with, to call his name from across the playground and smile, thump his back, crowd around him in a pack and head into the school building like brothers, like he was just part of the team.

Oh, well.

Even when he was fine, Calvin never had that. He has always watched from the sidelines. And now, well, he hasn't been in school for two months. A couple of kids have called, but not many.

I slapped my cheeks to snap myself out of it and slid down the banister, determined not to be grim. Last thing he needs.

When I got down to the kitchen, he was sitting there already, his new clothes draped around his skeletal frame, trying to fake a smile for our mother, who had a pan of scrambled eggs in her hand. She was smiling, too, but the tightness around her eyes wasn't fooling anyone.

"We've only got five minutes," I reminded her.

"I thought I could, you know, drive you guys

today," she said, spooning some eggs onto my plate and Calvin's.

"Oh," I said. "Okay."

Calvin poked at the toast on his plate. "You don't have to," he said to me. "You can take the bus."

"Are you kidding?" I was talking louder than I needed to, like Dad, lately, when he talks to Calvin. "A ride is sweet!"

Calvin and Mom both flinched. I smiled to show I was psyched, definitely pumped up about getting a ride. Oh, yes, this day is going surprisingly well! Everything is great!

I was scaring them both, I could tell, with my manic, lunatic grin and wide-open eyes. Okay, I was scaring myself, too. I took a huge bite of eggs on toast to move the breakfast along, change the mood.

"See?" Mom coaxed. "Jodie's eating, Calvin. Come on, have some."

My eggs suddenly felt rubbery in my mouth. *Leave him alone*, I thought. I couldn't swallow.

Calvin picked up about a molecule of egg on his fork and placed it in his mouth. "It's delicious," he said.

"Just two bites, Calvin," Mom pleaded. "Two good bites. You need some protein. Please."

Though it felt like the egg in my mouth had suddenly re-formed itself inside its hard shell, I managed to choke it down. I gasped for air as my mother sighed, so Calvin picked up another speck on a tine of his fork and dropped it into his mouth.

"Atta boy," my father told Calvin, in his Pep-Talk Dad voice. "Way to get your strength back. Knock 'em dead today, son."

"Okay," Calvin replied meekly.

My parents shot each other a look. Then Mom put her smile on again as she grabbed her keys from the hook and said, "Okeydokey, smokies! Let's skedaddle!"

Calvin and I followed her through the mud room to the car.

I sat in back and let Calvin take the front so he wouldn't get carsick on the way to school. Sinking down with my knees against the back of his seat, I willed some of my strength into him. *Please be strong, Calvin. Don't . . . just don't . . .*

Oh, please, just don't let people stare. Please, let everybody just ignore him like they used to. No whispering. No pointing. No guidance counselor with her fake nodding and smiling—please don't let her be waiting for him to make sure he is okay. Just let him be invisible like he used to be.

Mom slowed the car down and pulled up outside the fence. She turned to Calvin and quietly asked, "Should I walk you in?"

"No," he said, opening his door.

"Sure?" She attempted a smile again.

"We'll be fine," I assured her, getting out. Calvin and I slammed our car doors shut at the same time. "Ready?" I asked him.

He shrugged.

I nodded. No fake smiles. "Let's go."

We walked into the playground, where most of the kids already were, because the buses get there by 8:05, and it was already about a quarter past. I could hear Calvin beside me trying to take deep, cleansing breaths like his therapist had suggested. By habit, my eyes scanned the playground for Mackey, even though of course I wasn't going to go off and leave Calvin alone. Not today.

Over by the far hoop, my eye stopped on someone, and it took me a second to realize why—the kid had a bald head. Weird. Maybe there was somebody else going through chemo and I didn't know about it. Guess I'd been too wrapped up in my own family's pain to notice, or even to remember, that we didn't invent this—this ache, this tragedy. It's so easy to feel sorry for myself, for us, to sink into the feeling that we're the only ones who ever got dealt an unlucky hand.

We were heading in that direction, but I purposely looked away. That kid didn't need people staring at him, either.

"Calvin!" I heard Mackey bellow. "Yo, Cal!"

I had to smile, just hearing his voice. The guy has a set of lungs, for sure. Calvin and I looked around for him and stopped dead in our tracks when we saw what was coming at us.

It was Mackey, though it took me a second to figure that out. His grin gave him away. He was waving, grinning, flanked by six of his buddies from the soccer team. They were heading straight toward us, with their long, loping, soccer-boy swaggers, shoulder to shoulder, covering the distance between us fast.

And here's the thing: They were bald.

I don't mean crew cuts. All seven boys had completely shaved their heads.

They surrounded us.

"Hey," these bald, barely recognizable boys I've known half my life said to my brother. "Hey, Cal," and "Hi," and "What's up?"

Calvin didn't say anything. His mouth hung open a little, then curved into a small smile.

"What do you say we bust outta here?" Mackey asked him. "Go have some fun, shoot some pool, make some noise?"

Calvin's face tensed, so I said, "Mackey . . ."

"All right, all right, let's take over the school, then. Right, guys?"

"Yeah," a few of them grunted.

"Yeah," said Calvin, too.

"Much!" Mackey yelled, and slung his big arm over Calvin's narrow shoulders. The pack of bald boys turned and strode toward the front door of school together. I couldn't even see Calvin squashed in among them. I couldn't move. I just watched them go.

# Be Careful What You Wish For

**by Jane Yolen and Heidi E. Y. Stemple**

Every story I ever read—and I read a lot—says that being granted a wish is dangerous. Even the good wishes. Like wanting someone dead to come alive again, or asking for world peace. But I always thought: Surely I'd be smart enough to figure it out. To ask for just the right wish in just the right words.

Yeah, and I'm the Queen of England. (No, I didn't wish for that.) All I wished for was that my mother and father would be happy together. You wouldn't believe what a mess that turned out to be.

I thought I needed just one small wish—nothing elaborate—nothing that would change the past, which is usually the kiss of death. Just a bit of help to work out the future. I understand that you can't just pop back in time and fix things that happened without big consequences. I believe in magic. Not miracles.

Now, it's important that you know I'm closing in on my black belt in karate. Next year I'm going to learn the brick-smashing hand chop. My sensei, who also teaches at a college, told me that breaking the brick has nothing to do with magic and everything to do with physics. The secret, he said, is about the speed and focus of the strike.

Speed and focus—that's what I was working on in karate.

But what I was really working on right then was trying not to cry—which is such a wimpy thing, and I'm not that kind of girl.

That fateful afternoon, on the last day of summer before seventh grade, my parents had just told my sister, Joanne, and me that, after years of snapping at each other—morning snaps and evening snaps and gingersnaps and all—they were separating. Getting a divorce.

"We'll all be much happier for it," Mom said, her hands wrangling together. "And after all, happiness is important."

All! As if Joanne and I were included in that

happiness. But we were used to the snapping and the cold stares and the simmering anger. I mean, that was just what moms and dads did, as far as we knew. So why now? Why separate now?

Dad just looked relieved that she'd said it, not him. I bet they drew straws to see who was going to tell the kids.

I can't say I was shocked. Maybe stunned. No, not stunned. Maybe just ticked off that no one had asked me. Just delivered a message, a fiat, a law.

So I went outside, to the gray Goshen stone steps that led down from our house to the river below. Well, not a river. More like a stream with attitude. There was a stone bench that my dad had built years ago, when he was still doing that sort of thing for the house, for us. I sat down, bit my lip to keep from crying, then slammed my karate hand, focusing the strike, and said the word.

No, I can't tell you which word, but it was a bad one. *The* bad one. When I bashed the stone bench, I have to admit I did weep a single tear. Well, maybe more than one. Because honestly, I hadn't yet learned how to focus quite enough, and I was afraid I'd broken my hand, which was all I needed on top of the separation.

And then the strangest thing happened.

Something started to form, like clay on a pottery

wheel, growing higher and higher. Well, maybe not clay, more like smoke. Well, actually the something began swirling, like dust motes in the air.

A huge deep voice spoke to me. "Who ... called ... the ... genius ... loci?"

At first I thought it said it was a genie. That was before I had taken Latin in high school, so how was I to know it meant it was the genius (spirit) of the loci (place)?

I called it Genie.

Did I mention it was BIG?


Okay. Now here is where things got seriously weird. As if a sixteen-foot genie wasn't weird enough.

First, I have to tell you that when something like this happens, you would think that you'd question it in your mind. But you don't. It's simply there. Period. End of sentence. There is no shaking your head to try to clear it. There are no funny screen effects. And no one is waiting behind a tree to claim they'd just punked you. I didn't worry that I was seeing things, or hallucinating, or having a stroke. I don't do drugs or alcohol, and I am not a narcoleptic nor a schizophrenic, nor do I have fits. The thing just WAS.

"Er," I called, "hello, Genie." My voice was stronger than I'd have thought possible under the circumstances, though still a good deal higher than I normally speak. Not what you'd call a great opening. Not even a good one. But at least our conversation began.

I explained what I was wishing for. And the genius loci listened from high above me. I wouldn't call what he did active listening, all those things that teachers teach you about, like nodding your head or keeping eye contact or asking pointed questions. But I knew that he was taking in every little bit of my predicament. It had to do with his stillness, if a sixteen-foot creature out of myth could be said to be still. Rather, he quietly wafted above me. Or not wafted, exactly, but waved. Well, not really waved, but quietly swirled.

I thought as my story was unfolding that I was saved! My family was saved! Joanne and I would not become statistics, another two kids from a broken family, but remain part of an intact, if bickering, whole.

I had a lot to learn about magic.

The tears had dried on my cheeks, and I was ready to make the actual Big Wish, ready to smile.

"You see," I concluded, "I know my parents can work it out. So my wish, dear Genie, is that because many parents stay together for the good of the children ... I mean, I'm their children. Well, Joanne and me, we're their children. My parents. Not the many parents. And this is what's good for me. For us. They'll understand once you fix things."

I was breathless with anticipation as I gazed up at him. Well, not exactly gazed, but gawked, or rather gaped at his wafting, whirling, sixteen-foot presence. But who ever could have guessed that my problem solver, my prayer answerer, this genius of this most beautiful loci, could be so dense?

His voice spiraled down to me like wind through the trees, his opening mouth a darker part of his swirling grayness. "Alas, I cannot be of help to you, young lady," he said. "It is not my department." As if wish granting was under some kind of governmental bureaucracy.

I was so astonished that I nearly toppled off the bench—on which, apparently, I'd stood up in the midst of my explanation. And this was quite a shock because, in my karate class, I'm known for my impeccable balance, if not my focus.

"De—de . . . part . . . ment?" I stuttered.

He bent over till we were eye to eye, my blue eyes boring into his cloud-colored eyes. "Little mistress," he explained slowly, as if talking to a child or someone hard of hearing, "a genius loci cannot be called upon for such small favors. We do not manipulate interpersonal relationships. A genius loci is of higher stature than the fixers of these small problems. A genius loci is summoned to deal with matters of biblical proportions: great floods, devastating tornadoes, catastrophic maelstroms." He laughed, a small mountain of sound. "On the other hand, little mistress, an actual genie builds castles, finds lost princesses, does away with wicked viziers. A master wizard can find buried treasure, change straw into gold." He took a breath that sounded like the beginning of a thunderstorm, all whoosh and swoosh.

I stood motionless on the bench, mouth agape.

"Kid," he said to me, twirling faster, "you need another kind of wish granter."

And, poof—I mean really \*\*\* POOF \*\*\*—in a cloud of lavender smoke, he was gone.

The next morning I found myself still in my clothes, on top of my blankets, not remembering even having gone to bed. I was thinking about the wish. And suddenly, there was a small knock on my window.

This may not seem odd to anyone living in a ranch-style house, all on one floor. But I live in the converted attic of a 120-year-old Victorian farmhouse—well, half a Victorian farmhouse. It is split down the middle now, and we live in half of it and rent the other half—which is empty right now since the little old lady who used to live there moved to Florida. My room is under the eaves. And the only window in my room is a dormer three stories up. Not a knock-able window by a long shot.

On occasion I get birds and bats, but no knocking-on-the-window visitors.

So why I even went to look is beyond me. Though, perhaps because of the events of the day before, I was willing to give anything a shot. I flung open the window expecting, I guess, a bird or bat attempting to nest on the ledge.

What I was not expecting was . . . her.

But in she glided on shimmering wings. All pink and sparkly and shedding glittery starlike thingies. Did I mention PINK? She was the girliest thing I had EVER seen. And I have a six-year-old sister who lives and dies princesses, so I've seen some pretty girlie things.

Once the twinkly dust had cleared and this glit-tery girlie creature had landed, I could see she was old—though old like mom and dad, not like the old lady from next door—with long golden curls and brown eyes lined with silver and light-blue sparkles. She wasn't fairy-tale beautiful, but her face was like my sister's kindergarten teacher's, sweet-looking. Well, not sweet exactly, but charming. Well, not charming really, but kind. Her skirts, which seemed to have a mind of their own, swirled around a bit before settling, and the billowy, shimmering wings followed suit.

And then she somehow took a step toward normal, though still very pink. I had a fleeting thought about having to explain why there was a strange woman in my room—and no one could be stranger—but it passed quickly as this creature opened her mouth.

"Hello, Betsy, I'm your fairy godmother." She practically sang the greeting, all tinkling bells and harp chords.

"I prefer Liz, actually."

She smiled.

"Okay by me, Lizzy. I've been sent to help you with your big problem."

I gulped. "My big problem."

"You know—marriage, divorce, separation, grief. Families are my business."

"Your *department*?" I asked.

She gave me her sweet, charming, kind smile. "Exactly," she said.

"Oh, yikes," I moaned. Fairy godmothers are for princesses and little girls. I'm about to enter middle school. I'm practically already a black belt in karate. I don't like pink. I don't do sparkles. Even at Halloween, I'm a pirate or a swordswoman or Mia Hamm.

But, then, reality—or what was my new and strange reality—set in.

"Do I get wishes?"

"Don't be greedy, Lizzy. You get just the one," she said. "So think about it carefully."

"I've already thought about it. A lot!" I told her. Well, maybe not a lot, but quite a bit. Or at least some.

"With wishes, one has to be . . ." she began, but seeing that my face was set, she nodded. "All right, dizzy Lizzy, go ahead."

I took a deep breath, ignoring the nickname I hated, and let it all come out at once. The wish. The one I'd thought about.

"I really just want us all to be happy together," I said. "Dad, Mom, Sis, and me. No more snapping, snarling, or cold silences."

"Is that it?" she asked, wand upraised.

I thought about what I'd just said, examined it for possible hiccups. It wasn't enough for us just to be together. That would have been a stupid wish. After all, we'd been together and Mom and Dad hadn't been happy for a long time. If the fairy godmother put us back together and we were still unhappy, they'd just separate again. I'd figured that out on my own.

Sighing deeply, I said, "That's it. I just want us all to be happy together, Dad, Mom, Sis, and me."

She smiled, and it seemed a pretty real and kind smile. The wand waved over me, spreading its sparklies everywhere. "Good wish."

"Thanks," I said, mightily relieved.

I should have known better.

At breakfast the next morning, the wish seemed to be working well. My mom made pancakes, and my dad made my sister's lunch for her first day in first grade. I made my own, of course.

Stunningly, there was no fighting, no ugly looks. They even talked a bit.

I'd say it seemed like old times, but old times had never been as nice as this. Not for as long as I could remember.

There was no sign of the fairy godmother, which was just as well because, let's face it, showing up for the first day of seventh grade with her in tow would mean certain social death. The genius loci? Well, maybe he would be cool. Even awesome. But not that sparkly, pink creature. Not even if she granted wishes to all of my friends.

I climbed into the back seat of Dad's SUV, feeling quite full of myself. After all, I was the one who'd made all this happiness happen. Even if no one else in the family knew.

Mom kissed my sister good-bye. Joanne climbed

into the backseat next to me, scrambling into her car seat. No kisses for me, of course. I'd put an end to that practice two years ago when Mom tried to kiss me in front of all my soccer mates on my first day of fifth grade. Still, she gave me a big grin and started to say something.

At that very moment, Joanne, normally a pretty quiet kiddo, suddenly started babbling something to Dad about the new first-grade teacher who was *so* different from her kindergarten teacher in that he was a boy. He'd come to her kindergarten room on the last day of school last June, or something.

But her babbling didn't annoy me because everyone seemed happy. Wonderful. Even perfect. The wish had worked!

*Seemed.* Magic is always full of seemings. And twistiness. In all the stories, that's how it is. And here I thought we'd gotten off easy. That I had made a wish that couldn't be messed up.

Happy. Wonderful. Perfect. That is, until my dad slammed on the brakes halfway down the driveway. I couldn't see what was going on because we were in reverse and I was head down in my backpack trying to find my iPod, to drown out my sister's babbling. But the screeching of the tires, coming to a complete and speedy halt, jarred me out of my search. My first thought was that Dad had run over the For Rent sign again that announced we were looking for a new tenant for the empty side of the house.

No such luck.

Instead, the passenger door opened, and in slid my pink fairy godmother.

My dad looked shocked as she closed the door, careful not to capture all that pink froofy fabric in it. She turned to wink at me. I did not wink back. I just stared, mouth open, eyes wide. Dumbstruck, actually.

Then she turned to my dad. I hoped upon hope that she would take out some sort of wand, bop him on the head, and all this divorce nonsense would be over. At the same time, I hoped upon hope that she was not actually staying in the car and accompanying us to school. I was sure that I couldn't survive her being seen with my dad.

As it turned out, I was pointing my hopes in the wrong direction.

When their eyes met, something happened. All that funny music—the stuff that had carried my fairy godmother in through the window the night before—started to swirl around them. Birds and butterflies actually flew above their heads. They both got this gooshy look at the exact same time.

Dad smiled. He sighed.

I almost threw up onto my iPod.

"What the—" I'm pretty sure I said that out loud. Not the swear word at the end, but what comes right before it. My dad snapped out of whatever spell he was under and turned to say something to me.

The fairy godmother unbuckled her seat belt, turned around in the seat, and fixed me with a look that froze me. Well, actually, it didn't freeze me, but it did literally freeze my dad, my sister, the car, and everything around it for at least a block away, including the trees and a stupid blue jay flying toward a pine tree in our front yard. In fact, I was the only thing not frozen.

I decided to use that to my advantage.

"What the heck are you doing to me? To my dad? With my dad?" My mouth began to run away with me. Run? It was positively galloping. I took a breath and continued. "You are supposed to be getting Mom and Dad back together, not going googly-eyes and butterflies with him. Do you think this is a date? Do you think this is a joke? You're the worst fairy godmother in the history of fairy godmothers. In fact, I think I will have to report you to the fairy godmother board. If there is such a thing. Or maybe I'll just call in that big guy, the genius not genie. He must be in charge of something!"

"Whoa, there, little woman," she said, stopping me in mid-rant. "Remember your wish?"

Of course I remembered. "I really just want us all to be happy together: Dad, Mom, Sis, and me. No more snapping, snarling, or cold silences," I told her.

"And where in that wish does it say, 'No dating my father'? Or even, 'My parents have to remain married'?"

My jaw dropped. "It was assumed."

"Magic never assumes anything," she said, leaning over the seat until we were practically nose to nose. "In fact, magic is more technical than the law. It's precise. That's the first thing we learn in fairy god-mother school."

I snuffled. "But two people happy together will stay married."

"Are you married to your best friend, George? Am I married to my best friend, the genius loci? Happiness belongs to itself and is not dependent on marriage, cohabitation, or even for the people involved to be living in the same biosphere."

I hadn't a clue as to what she was talking about, except that being-married-to-my-best-friend-George business, which was too ooky even to contemplate.

And it was much too late to say any more because the world around us started moving, or spinning, again. But it all seemed to be happening without me. Though this was supposed to be a big day for me—

my first in middle school—all I could do was walk through it like a zombie.

When the bus dropped me off at the end of my street (that's the deal—I suffer through the parental drop-off in the morning and get to take the bus home), I contemplated walking the other way. Away from my house, my family, and my troubles. I figured I could just keep walking and stop when I got to some other house in some other state with a family that would take me in. Surely there had to be good families who wanted an almost-black-belt refugee from a broken home.

Breaking into this daydream was my fairy godmother. Well, not her in person, but her presence. I could hear her tinkling laugh—well, not hear it exactly, but I could sense it hovering over my house. Now I had to go home, if for no other reason than to break up the merriment between her and my dad. I mean, really.

But it wasn't my dad my fairy godmother was with at my house. She and my mom were sitting on the back porch sipping tea and having a giggling girl talk. What was it Alice said when she fell down the rabbit hole? *Curiouser and curiouser.* Well, how much curiouser could my life get?

I peeked my head out the door. Mom didn't see me, but my backstabbing fairy godmother gave me one of those looks that made me know not to disturb them. It didn't tell me to go away, exactly. But there was a large suggestion in that look. Well, maybe just a strong hint. So I ducked back into the house but left the door open so I could listen.

And that was when things got even more tangled.

"You are so right, Gloria," Mom was saying. "He is a dreamy creature."

My dad—dreamy? Maybe I had misjudged the FGM. I almost burst back through the door to thank her. But the next thing I heard stopped me cold.

"He certainly is, Merry," the FGM answered. "Can you imagine someone that yummy teaching first grade?"

Oh, for creep's sake, they were talking about Mr. Colton, my sister's teacher! I ran to the bathroom, thinking about washing out my ears or showering in ice-cold water. Anything—ANYTHING—to get the taste and sound of those words out of my skull.

After a few minutes, I calmed down enough to think straight. Or as straight as I'd been thinking the last couple of days.

There was only one thing left to do. And I did it.

I marched out to the gray Goshen steps and the stone bench. I sat down and thought for a moment about what I needed to say. Then I slammed my karate hand on the stone, focusing the strike, and said the word. Not once. Not twice. But three times. I was not going to take any chances that the genius loci was going to ignore me.

This time I was pretty sure I'd broken my hand. But that wasn't going to stop me from doing what I had to do.

Sure enough, the gray twirling misty stuff rose up, and soon Mr. Sixteen-Feet-Tall-and-Counting was peering down at me.

"I told you, young lady, Happy Families Is Not My Department," he said. "Unless you now have a serious whirlwind, maelstrom, or earthquake to report, leave me alone."

I smiled through the pain. Well, actually, the smile was painful, too. "What I have to say is serious enough to rock your world." I took a deep breath. "The fairy godmother has fallen for my father."

"Fallen? Is she hurt?"

I had to laugh. "Fallen as in gone for, done for, enamored of, in love with a human."

That stopped him twirling.

I thought he would blow. I was pretty sure there would be some sort of natural disaster to follow—

maybe even a tornado that would lift up the house and set it down right on top of that witch of a fairy godmother. Perhaps there would even be flying monkeys.

A noise stopped my reverie, and I realized I'd been holding my breath. Must be thunder crackling in preparation for the oncoming storm. I looked up, expecting to see clouds darkening the sky, purple streaks, trees bending in the wind.

But it was just the genius. He was not ratcheting up for a hurricane, not even a good old-fashioned New England electrical storm. He was ...

He was laughing.

LAUGHING!

And finally, when he got the words out around the gales of giggles, he said, "Not My Department!"

Almost one year later, actually, just one day short—the last day of the next summer—my sister shouted up to me that the barbecue was ready. The yard was now twice its size since my dad had ripped down the fence when he moved into the old lady's house next door.

I grabbed my black belt from the top of my dresser and tied it around me. I wanted to wear it because the barbecue was a celebration of my big achievement.

As I came into the yard, the air smelled of burgers and dogs. My mom was manning the grill, and my dad was fussing with the salads on the picnic table.

Mr. Colton—well, I call him Bob now—was tossing a baseball to my sister while his dog, Murray, ran barking between the two of them.

I sat down next to Gloria, whom I just refer to as FGM. I never did like the concept of stepmother, so we just keep it simple. She was still in pink, but now it was a huge pink dress to cover her very pregnant belly—soon to be my baby brother.

We both sat quietly and watched the family for a little while. Actually, though we never talk about it directly, I know she's given up her magic for this. That's positively the bravest thing I've ever heard of. I hope she doesn't regret it, but I'm always afraid to ask. I don't want to spoil it. For her. Or for me.

It may not have been what I had intended to wish for a year ago, but in the end, it was exactly right.

FGM leaned over and patted me on the knee. She may be out of magic, but she still seems to be able to read my mind. I was sure I could hear the tinkling bells when she said, "Not only happy together, Lizzy, but happily ever after."

And I believe her. Entirely.

# Beggar's Ride

### by A. LaFaye

My mom always said, "If wishes were horses, beggars would ride." Sounded good to me. I always wanted a horse. And, in our last week of summer vacation, I planned to use that horse to ride away from a couple of beggars. Not just any beggars, but my twin brothers, the worst two whiners in the second grade, the whole town of Middleburg, Minnesota, and the entire tristate area.

We'd been on the road since dawn, and all I could hear was, "Let's stop for ice cream!" "Come on, Dad, we've got to and see the biggest ball of string in the world." "How about we just drive to Canada and play hockey?" "I have to go potty." "I want a candy bar" ... "buffalo jerky" ... "a pencil sharpener in the shape of the state". . . .

I'll tell you what *I* wanted. I wanted my wish to come true so bad my toes ached from trying to cross them. I *wish* I never have to take another vacation in a car with these begging machines.

Who takes a vacation to Iowa, anyway? I mean, Iowa is a place you get away *from*, not get away *to*. Families take vacations to Disneyland or Busch Gardens. I'd even take the Mall of America. At least there I could get away from Attila the Horrible and his twin, Alexander the Grape for Brains.

Their real names are Atticus and just plain Alexander, after Atticus Finch in *To Kill a Mockingbird* and Alexander Graham Bell. See, my dad loves books and my mom loves science.

How else could I have ended up with a name like Brontë Curie Wells? Yeah, that's right, I'm named after a bunch of writing sisters and a woman who helped discover radium. Don't ask me what that is. I just know it can kill you if you work with it too long. That's what happened to the real Curie. But I'd even eat the stuff right now if it would get me away from the Twin Tornadoes. They've already got death on their minds with Dad's grand plan to search every graveyard from Minneapolis to Des Moines to find lost relatives.

I could think of a few relatives we should lose. Why do we need to find dead ones we've never met?

"Let's go to that graveyard tonight!" Atticus yelled for the fortieth time in two minutes. "We've got flashlights." He tested one out by turning it on and off right in my face.

"Not this time, Buster," Mom said, still trying to fold the map she'd been fighting with since we got off the highway. "I'm not pulling you out of another grave."

"That was cool!" Alexander yelled. "His leg sank into the ground—*kerplush*—right into that rotted old coffin. Did you feel dead bones with your toes?"

Atti started kicking wildly, like he felt himself sinking into that grave all over again. And to set the record straight, *I* pulled that little creep, kicking and screaming, out of that sunken grave. Let me tell you, it sold me on aluminum caskets. Those wood ones just rot away and bring a whole new meaning to the idea of a death trap.

"I still think you should've gone back for your shoe. But you were too *scared*," Alex said, taking off his smelly old shoe and shoving it toward Atti. "Afraid of a little shooo ..."

"Get it away!" Atti shoved it back.

"Ew," Alex teased, shoe wagging.

"Get it away!" Atti said again.

As we pulled into a motel, I grabbed the shoe and threw it out the window. "It's away," I said.

Atti started to laugh.

Alex began to whine. "Mom, Brontë—"

I snatched Atti's flashlight and shined it right in Alex's eyes, whispering, "Tell her and I'll let her know you're the one who used her new raincoat for a slip and slide."

But he didn't need a threat. He'd already bolted out the door, yelling, "I call the remote!"

"No, I do!" Atti said, and scrambled after him.

I collapsed against the seat, letting Mom and Dad get the luggage, check in, and send Alex after his shoe.

I'd get maybe ten minutes to work on my sketches before everyone got to our room and hit battle mode. So I took my tablet and pencils and waited for the Two Typhoons to swirl in and open the door. Then I took up my post in front of the window as they scrambled to find the remote.

"Where is it?"

"Did you steal it?"

Dad came in, waving the remote over his head. "No TV until you've both read for an hour, quietly and without hurting each other." Slipping the remote into his pocket and dropping the luggage off his shoulders, Dad hopped onto the bed he'd share with Mom and opened his own book.

The boys started to whine.

Dad held up his hand. "Every complaint adds five minutes. You're up to an hour and ten by now."

With eye rolls and carpet scuffing, they went to their corners. And I actually got to draw a little. I figured I might even have a sliver of a chance of completing my portfolio by the October 1 deadline to get into the Harrington Academy of the Arts for spring semester—a whole five states away from the Hun and the Grape. No way could those hooky-loving, detention-getting, D-graders ever get into a private arts school. But I had a shot. Getting in could mean I'd become the most famous sixth-grader in town. The closest anybody in my grade got to artistic talent was Bennie Larsen winning the coloring contest at Cub Foods. But I had to finish the portfolio first.

The A Team had already tried to destroy my chances. Those crude creeps even tore up my first ten drawings to make snow for their reenactment of the Battle of the Bulge. They ripped up any piece of paper they could find, then set it all flying with every fan in the house running in their room until they blew a fuse and got sentenced to doing yard work for a month. Now we have bald hedges and a crew-cut lawn with a skull etched into the backyard, and I'm still five drawings short.

I had just enough time to put a few finishing

touches on a sketch of my friend Kelli on her horse, midjump, if those two could keep quiet for even a quarter of the time Dad had asked them to . . . Wait a minute. It is quiet. Too quiet. Mom's reading her science journal and Dad's deep in his novel—and the boys are . . . gone, their comic books on the floor where they left them.

Who cares? Let them sneak out and get caught. More drawing time for me. I went back to work.

But within seconds, other noises began to bother me; the squeaking brakes of a semitruck rolling in, someone next door playing the news channel too loud, murder this, robbery that. Then two guys started to argue in the parking lot.

"Rowdy place," Mom said to Dad, without looking up.

Rowdy? This place sounded dangerous to me. The boys could get hurt. Not scrape-the-knee, knock-on-the-noggin hurt, but kidnapped or killed kind of hurt.

"Where are the boys?" I asked.

"They're right—" Mom turned away from her magazine. Seeing that they'd left, she dropped the magazine and went into disaster mode, yelling, "Robert!"

Dad jumped off the bed and made it to the bathroom in two strides. "Boys?"

"I'll check the car." Mom ran for the door.

"I'll loop around the motel," I said, hopping down.

"No, you don't, Brontë." Dad sat me down on the bed. "If this place isn't safe for them, it's not safe for you. You wait here in case they come back."

Dad checked the alley. Mom headed for the front desk. I looked under the beds and in the shower to be sure they weren't playing a practical joke. I even scanned the roof with a flashlight, in case they'd climbed up there. Those yahoos would go anywhere and do anything.

Last summer, when we did the graveyard tour of South Dakota, the boys sneaked off from the hotel. We found them by the pool, selling candy. They claimed the candy had *fallen out* of a vending machine when a football player smashed it for stealing his dollar.

I ran out to check every last vending machine at the motel. No boys.

By the time I got back to our room, the management had started a room-to-room search with my parents, who told me to stay in the room. But each time I heard them knock on a door it rattled my heart—my mind seeing two police officers standing there to say they had bad news.

I might hate their punching, despise their dirty tricks, and want them to shrink to the size of crickets so I could feed them to their pet snake, but I have never really wanted anything bad to happen to the twins.

Not this bad, anyway.

So when I remembered how much they wanted to see that nearby cemetery, I knew I had to go find them. I left a note for Mom and Dad and made a bee-line for the cemetery. Rain started falling as I ran past Uncle Mel's House of Pancakes and headed for the empty lot beyond it. As I sloshed through the tall grass, I swept the beam of my flashlight over the path ahead. I could see the trees along the edge of the cemetery, dead ahead.

"Alex, Atti!" I shouted. No answer. Those little creeps would never answer me, but I kept calling anyway.

I charged through the cemetery, shouting and stumbling like an idiot. But all I found were shadows, a stray cat, and a family of raccoons heading for a stream I could hear just beyond the cemetery.

Did the boys go there? They wouldn't if they had brains. Both of them had flunked out of swimming lessons for fooling around in the pool.

I had visions of Atticus chasing Alex over the rocks, Atti slipping and falling, hitting his head, and sliding into the water, Alex fighting to pull him out before they both got dragged downstream. . . .

I rushed in to find that the water barely came up

to my ankles. Even swimmers as bad as my brothers could get out of that puddle of a stream. So where did those creeps go? The rain made the opposite bank so slick that I had to pull myself to the top. I called their names from the bluff. "Alex! Atti!"

Still no answer.

Unless you count the strobe flash of lightning that lit up the open field ahead, outlining an abandoned house that stared back at me like a cracked old skull.

I jumped.

*It's just a house, Brontë. And a creaking old windmill.*

But not to the boys. No, sir. That place would be a magnet to those treasure hunters. I ran straight for it, calling out as the wind picked up and the rain started to come down hard enough to make everything blurry.

The door kept slamming in the wind with a splintery thud, keeping an odd beat with the scraping turn of the windmill. Beyond that, I heard something else—fainter, harder to hear. Was it sheep bleating?

No. I could hear it now.

"Help!"

The boys.

"Atticus? Alexander?" I ran harder, even with the rain doubling the weight of my clothes.

"Brontë! We fell."

I shot my light down but saw only wet grass whipped by the wind. "Where?"

"The well!"

Oh, no! They'd fallen into the well pumped by that rusted old windmill. I ran, but the ground got all slippery and slanted as I got closer. Then my feet slid toward a muddy black hole. I grabbed the support of the windmill just as my legs slid over the edge. The windmill creaked against my weight. I thought my arms would snap out of my shoulders as I dangled into the well.

"Grab my feet!" I shouted.

"You're too far up!" Atticus yelled.

"Hurry, Brontë. There's water. Lots of water."

That water probably broke their fall, but with all the rain coming down it would soon do more harm than good. And those two goof-offs couldn't swim! Scrambling back to solid ground, I yelled down, "I'll go get Mom and Dad!"

"Don't leave!"

Shining the light down, I could see their pale faces above the water and their arms slicing through it like fish. "Can you touch the bottom?"

"No!"

And those two couldn't tread water for long. I'd never get to the motel and back before they gave up.

"I'll find something." I ran to the abandoned house. I knew that any rope I found would be too old to hold their weight.

Inside, I yanked doors open, knocked over furniture, pulled out drawers, and tried to find something—anything—I could use to help them. A kitchen drawer broke, clattered to the floor, and sent rusted metal clanking across the old linoleum.

Silverware.

Knives.

If I couldn't pull my brothers out, maybe they could climb out.

I scrambled to find four knives. Thunder boomed above me, and lightning charged the room with light. *One knife. Two. Fork. Spoon. Spoon. Three. Fork, fork, fork, what? No more knives? Wait. There's one under the table! Four.*

Yanking the sweater off my back, I dropped down beside the well and scrambled to tie the knives up. "Swim to the sides," I called. "I'm throwing down a sweater!"

"A sweater! What good is that going to do?"

I dropped it, shouting, "Just grab it quick."

They jumped at the sweater as soon as it hit the water and tugged away at it.

"Get the knives," I said.

"Knives?" Atticus's voice popped and gurgled as they fought to get a knife and stay afloat.

"Dig in, boys. Climb the wall."

"Yeah!" they shouted together, catching on.

I could see them digging in and edging up. "I told Mom I should've brought my baseball cleats!" Alex shouted.

I heard an *ouch* from Alex, and Atticus shouted, "I dropped a knife!" *Splash*. It hit the water. He fell back in with a loud *splash*.

"Atti!" Alex called.

"Keep climbing. Keep climbing," I yelled to Alex. "I'll find you something, Atti."

Racing back to the house, I spun on the porch like a cornered animal. What? What could I use? There were no more knives. Then, in the distance, I saw a shed. A shed that might have a trowel or a shovel, or a pick. Anything.

I ran out there, tossing rusted paint cans and wires out of my way.

*A screwdriver. I found a screwdriver. Two! And a file, and a trowel. Yes, yes, they'd work.*

I nearly fell over trying to make it back to the well fast enough, my new tools clanking back and forth in a paint can I'd picked up.

Both boys looked up at me from the bottom.

Alex shouted, "The knives are too weak. They can't hold us."

"Here comes more stuff—better stuff."

I dropped the can down the well.

*Please, please.* I wished so hard for it to work that I just about bit through my lip. Who knew if my parents would even think to look here? I swung my flashlight in a wide arc to shine the light in the air hoping they could see it, hoping they would think to look in the cemetery and know to keep searching.

Searching. That's what I had to do. Find something else to help the boys. I ran for the shed again, hoping to find something. But all I found was more wire, a lawn mower blade, and a broken hoe. Nothing.

*Wait, what's that? A hose. An old canvas fire hose. Now, that I could use!*

I looped one end around the windmill, pulling back on the hose to test its strength. It held. I heard one of the boys slip and hit hard against the wall.

"You okay, Atti?" Alex yelled.

"I'm coming!" I shouted.

Gripping the hose, I practically ran down the wall of that well. If I hadn't been so scared, I might've actually had some fun.

"Hey!" Alex yelled as he clung to me, just like he did after I rescued him from his attempt to swim across the Hemshaws' pool.

The extra weight sent me sliding farther down. I dug in my feet. But they slipped on the wet, muddy walls. The hose stretched and groaned. Could it hold us both?

"Get in front. Grab the hose."

As Alex climbed around, I held fast, my feet turning, my ankles aching. When he took hold of the hose in front of me, I said, "Hang tight!"

Working fast, I kicked off my shoes.

"What was that?" Atti called as they hit the water.

"Just shoes," I yelled, giving Alex a nudge. "Head up."

Now in my bare feet, I lowered myself down, knowing I had to get my weight off the hose but afraid to jump from that height.

"You coming?" Alex called.

"Keep going."

The hose didn't reach all the way to the water. Made me sick to my stomach to think of the sludgy water below. But I jumped.

*Ew.* The water felt like jumping into cold oil, all slimy and gross.

"Brontë?" they both yelled.

"Hey, who got first place in her last swim meet?"

"You," they answered.

I could hear Atti stabbing at the wall to get a hand-hold. But I couldn't see much, with all the rain and so little light.

"I'm up!" Alex shouted.

"Swing the hose around the edge until Atti can feel it!" I yelled.

I expected him to say, "So long, sucker." But he said, "Okay. Do you feel it?"

"No."

"Now?"

"No. Hey, hey, that was me!" Atti yelled. "Got it!"

I could hear him grunting and pulling like a mad little dog tugging on a toy.

Then Alex shouted, "You made it!"

I could hear them yelling and jumping.

"Come on up, Brontë!" They shone the flashlight down at me.

"Hose is too short," I yelled back.

Alex shone the light at Atti and then at me. "Too short?" he said.

They disappeared from the edge.

"Boys! Don't leave me here!"

I heard a slipping noise, like fabric coming down. Was that the hose? Did they drop it in? *Splunk.* Something hit the water. I expected to hear the whole thing spool in. But, no, it swished around like a snake fighting to get free.

"Grab it!" they shouted.

The hose flickered at the side of my face. I grabbed on. "Got it!"

They planned to pull me up themselves. No way.

I swam to the edge of the well, planted my feet, and started to climb up. *Please let the hose hold. Please let it hold.* What a beggar's ride this turned out to be! Me trudging and slipping my way up that well, the terrible twosome grunting and pulling and yanking. Bet they wished they had a horse to do the pulling then.

When I came out and collapsed on the ground, they dropped down to hug me and squeeze me and say something I'd never heard them say.

"We love you, Brontë."

I'd ride anywhere and give up almost any wish to hear those brats actually admit they liked having me around. But I had a hold over them now. They'd start acting up, and I'd say, "You need me to find a well to throw you in?"

And they'd laugh or punch me in the arm. Once Atticus even hugged me when I said that. But Alex went a little too far. Last week, Mom and Dad finally gave in to the boys' latest begging campaign—going to Disneyland for vacation. Because I'm home only for the holidays and summer break now that I'm officially a student at the Harrington Academy of the Arts—thank you very much. And that sounded good to me, but that little joker actually asked if we could drive instead of fly.

Oh, how I wish that won't happen.

# Star Light, Star Bright

## by Deborah Wiles

Today, on my first day at this new school, I made my first friend and I didn't have to lie. No, that's not true. I lied a lot. That's what started the whole thing. No, that's not true, either. A wish started it all. A wish for a friend.

My wish that we wouldn't have to move again had not been answered, like so many wishes that had gone unanswered in this, my twelfth year on the planet. So I'd wished for a friend.

I wore my lucky dish-ran-away-with-the-spoon pajamas as I stood barefoot in the weedy patch that was our new backyard at the Scarlett O'Hara Mobile Home Park outside of Athens, Georgia, on a cool November night, and I wished upon the first star. "Star light, star bright . . ."

And now here she was, my wish, leaning against my locker at lunchtime, a tall girl dressed in jeans and a sparkly silver sweater, her hair wild and sticking out on purpose all over her head, her skin as dark as the coffee my mama drinks on the way to work in the morning when she drops me off at school in a car that makes so much noise everyone stops to see who's getting out. That embarrasses me, although I don't say so. Mama has enough on her mind.

The girl in the silver sweater wore purple high-top sneakers with orange laces. She clasped her books across her chest in a haphazard way. If she'd been holding my baby brother, Henry, he would have slipped out of her grasp and—*squish!*—diaper-first, he would have plopped onto the polished tile floor like a soft cantaloupe. *Waaaaaaa!* That would have been a messy scene.

"Hey," the girl said as she moved out of my way so I could fumble with my lock. Kids swarmed around us, grabbing their lunches, banging shut their lockers, hailing one another with shouts of friendship. A free-for-all in the hallway.

"Hey," I said. I stared at my lock, trying to remember my combination. But all I could think was, *My wish! My wish! My wish has come true!*

"Work for what you want," Mama says. "Wishes have no power." She is so wrong.

I had no choice about moving—again—as I remind Mama every chance I get (I can't help it). I'm too young for a paying job, and besides, what does a friend cost? That's what I said to Mama.

"A true friend is a treasure more precious than gold," was all she said. Which said nothing. So I wished.

I have wished for a lot this year. I wished for Daddy to get better. He did, a little. I wished for the rent money. It didn't come. At my last school, I wished for Dave Devilbiss to like me, but he didn't. He called me a Salvation Army loser, but Mama said, "He's the loser, Berry," which didn't make me feel any better. "Stop wishing and start living," Mama said. I couldn't wait to tell her about my new friend and the real power of wishing—wouldn't she be surprised!

"You're new," said the girl. She popped her gum. I could feel her watching me twirl the knob around the combination lock.

"Yeah," I said. I wanted to look at her but I was afraid I'd grin like a stupid possum and maybe even say, "You were my wish!" Which would be so lame. I might even start telling the string of lies I told the

167

last time we moved. So I didn't look, and instead I wondered what star I had wished on. Maybe it had been a planet, such as Venus or even Jupiter.

"The locks don't work," said the girl. "Just yank on it." Which I did. But I did not want to open my locker. Not in front of this girl. I could not risk losing the only friend I had made in almost a whole year.

"My name's Glory," said the girl. "I saw you get out of that yellow car this morning. Where are you from?"

I stared at my sneakers. They were wrapped in duct tape and were two sizes too small.

"I'm Berry," I said, finally looking my new friend in the eye. "I'm from New York." Which was a lie.

Glory hooted. "Barry? That's a boy's name."

I pointed at my red hair. "Berry. Like strawberry."

"Oh," said Glory. "New York City?"

"Brooklyn, to be exact," I said. "Near the Brooklyn Bridge." I was good at this.

"Wow," said Glory. "Have you been to the top of the Empire State Building?"

"Lots of times," I said. "My father worked there before he got transferred to Athens."

I could have hugged myself. Glory was eyeing me with interest. "I've never been out of Georgia," she said. "Yet."

The bell rang. The hallway cleared. First-lunch began, and merriment spilled out of the cafeteria. The guidance counselor had shown me the cafeteria when she assigned me a buddy to walk with from class to class. My buddy got rid of me as soon as she could—I didn't even catch her name. The look she gave me told me everything I needed to know about this school. Kids at this school had things . . . and I didn't. These kids wouldn't want to know me; they never did. But now, here was Glory, my friend, walking right up to me like she knew I'd wished for her.

Glory shifted her books in her arms. "You buying lunch?"

"No," I said. "I brought from home."

"Well, come on," said Glory. "Grab your lunch, and I'll introduce you to some kids."

"Really?" That stupid possum grin spread across my face, anyway. I couldn't help it, but Glory didn't seem to mind.

"Yeah," she said. "You can tell us about New York City."

The last time I'd moved, I'd said I was from Los Angeles. LA. I'd been in a movie, too, I said, just as an extra. I made it sound real—I knew about Hollywood. Before we'd starting moving all over the place, we lived in Flowery Branch, an hour's drive from Athens, which is the big city. In Flowery Branch, I read all the movie magazines in the beauty parlor where I spent my after-school time with Miss Betty Jane Wilkins, who kept an eye on me while Mama and Daddy worked at Ben-Loc Poultry in Gainesville. My friend Lupe came with me. Her mama worked at Ben-Loc, too. Most folks did. Lupe and I mixed shampoo potions and helped Miss Betty Jane take out the perm rollers in customers' hair. We told knock-knock jokes and laughed ourselves silly about stupid boys.

But that was before Henry was born, before what happened to Daddy, and before we had to start moving. I blew out the candles on my last birthday cake—twelve, and one to grow on, almost a teenager—the same day we packed to move the third time.

Do you know how hard it is to keep in touch with friends when you move every three or four months? Lupe wouldn't know where to find me now, and I've lost her address. Even if I had it, what would I write to her about? How we move when we can't make the rent, so the landlord can't find us? How I might get new shoes this next paycheck? How we don't have an oven in this trailer, but it doesn't matter, Mama says, because we have heat? My friends in Flowery Branch hadn't known what to say to me when they found out I'd be leaving. I didn't know what to say to them. We'd had each other to laugh with just about all our lives. Now I had nobody.

"Hey, Glory!" A tall boy in a black jacket strutted by us. He wore a silver stud in his right earlobe. "Who's your friend?"

"She's Berry—like strawberry," said Glory. Her voice took on a pretend huff, like girls did with their voices when they were flirting: "Go on, Xavier, we've got no business with you!"

Xavier laughed. "Come to lunch, Strawberry!" he called as he sailed around the corner toward the cafeteria.

Oh! Two friends already! I squeezed my eyes shut tight. No one had been friendly in my last two schools. How I had wanted just one good friend! A friend to paint nails with, go to the movies with, bake cookies with, sing songs with, do homework with, kick a soccer ball with, play piano with, giggle over boys with. There was this one boy, Jeremy, in my next-to-last school. I think he liked me, but as soon as he really knew about me . . .

And if Glory knew about me? I didn't want to open my locker and spoil anything.

"I have to go to guidance," I lied. "They told me to come at lunch. I can meet you. I know where the cafeteria is."

Glory shrugged. "Suit yourself," she said. "Our

table's the third one on the left, near the bathrooms." She slouched off.

I took a deep breath. I knew nothing about New York or the Brooklyn Bridge. I knew everything about living with a father who had had a stroke and who didn't know me anymore and who packed my lunch so slowly, so carefully in a SpongeBob lunch box every day. It was the lunch box I'd used in kindergarten.

I opened my locker, flipped the lid on my lunch box, and lifted out the mayonnaise sandwich, the banana, and the water bottle I refilled every morning with water from the kitchen sink. I hurried to the lunchroom. No one mentioned my lack of a lunch bag.

Xavier looked me up and down. I had one small hole in the knee of my too-short jeans, and I wore a pilly green sweater that was several sizes too large.

"Great grunge look," said Xavier. "I bet that's popular in New York City, eh?"

I nodded with authority. "The grungier the better," I said. And I turned the conversation around, as I have learned to do—don't let anyone ask you too many questions. "What about you? You got sisters? Brothers?"

"Xavier is a mutant," said Glory. "He's from another planet."

Venus or Jupiter. Yes, I knew. He was cute, too.

Peanut-butter skin, dancing walnut eyes, freckles across his nose. I smiled at him. Smiled! His face colored up.

"Glory," I said, full of bravado, "do you like Johnny Depp?" Lupe and I had seen almost every Johnny Depp movie ever made. We even bought Dots at the theater, but never Jujubes. Jujubes stuck to our teeth too much.

"Listen!" shouted Glory. Kids were filling our table with their lunch trays and their noisy presence. "We've only got a week before Thanksgiving break, and we've got lots to decide. This is my new friend, Berry, like strawberry. She's from New York City, and she's going to help us."

I was dizzy with hellos and questions. "Help with what?" I asked.

But the kids had questions, too.

"Where's the meat in that sandwich?" asked Lucinda. Lucinda wore makeup. Lots of makeup.

"I like it like this," I said, trying to make sure my voice didn't tremble. Glory handed me a napkin. I put my sandwich in my lap.

Jennifer helped herself to my banana and began to open it with her manicured fingernails. "Could I have half?" she said. "It's nice to meet you, Berry. Great hair." My hair hung in a limp ponytail down my back.

"Soda machine's out of order," said Jake, shoving his swipe card into his pocket. "Who's got milk money I can borrow?"

Six kids slapped two quarters each on the table. With that many quarters I could buy a lunch, maybe two lunches. Jake went to fetch his milk. He had a haircut that screamed beauty parlor, and I thought of Lupe.

I opened my water and, with a long drink, summoned my courage. "Help with what?"

"One week until Thanksgiving break," said Glory, clapping her hands to bring order to the group. Her bracelets tinkled like tiny wind chimes. "The lunchtime meeting of the High-Minded Heroes will come to order."

I was in the club! I must have wished on the sun!

Kids ate their yogurt pretzels, ham sandwiches, and macaroni and cheese. They threw away their sliced carrots and green beans. I tore off small pieces of my mayonnaise sandwich and brought them to my mouth carefully. One thing I could say about Daddy these days, he made a mean mayonnaise sandwich.

"Xavier," directed Glory. "Read our mission statement, please."

I drained my water as Xavier obliged. "We, the High-Minded Heroes of Muscadine Middle School, are a group of kids who do noble deeds. We reach out to those less fortunate than we are. Every spring, we sponsor an Easter basket giveaway, and every November we give away an entire Thanksgiving dinner to a deserving, unfortunate family in need."

I couldn't help it; I spewed water all over myself and everyone else.

"Ew!" squealed Jennifer. She dropped my banana into her macaroni and cheese. Glory and Jake slapped me on the back until I waved my hands in a stop-it! motion.

"Come to order!" said Glory in a commanding voice. "We have work to do!"

I wiped my face with the napkin Glory had given me. "I'm so sorry," I mumbled. "I'm so sorry." I didn't know what else to say.

"No problem," said Glory. "Right?" She looked at all the other kids. They murmured their okays. I wasn't sure they meant it.

"I'm new," I said, as if that would make a difference and help me keep my friends.

"Yes," said Glory, "Berry is new, and she's from New York City, where there are lots of deserving families, aren't there, Berry?"

I nodded.

"Can you tell us how to spot them?" Glory asked. It seemed like a perfectly reasonable question.

I cleared my throat. "Well . . . I don't know," I said. "I—I went to private school in New York." I prayed they wouldn't ask me for the name of the school.

The bell rang. Kids began to pile up their trash on their trays and stand up.

"We need to meet outside of school!" said Glory. "We don't have enough time at lunch!" She gave me an earnest look. "Could we meet at your house this weekend, Berry?"

My stomach lurched. "No!" I blurted. "I'm—I'm not home this weekend!"

"You're not?" said Glory.

"No! No. We're going to—to Atlanta this weekend!" It was the biggest city nearby that I knew.

Xavier sidled up to me with his notebook in his hands. "Give us your telephone number and address, Berry, and we'll call you and make a date for our next meeting."

And—I couldn't believe that I did this, but I did it. I gave him my address. We don't have a phone, so I couldn't give him that. I told him I didn't remember my phone number yet. But I gave him my address and wanted to die. Why, why, why did I do that?

Because I had wished. I had wished for friends. And here they were. And so I wished some more. I wished we'd stay here, in this town, long enough for me to make friends. I wished Xavier would like me.

I wished Glory would understand when Xavier told her he liked me more than he liked her. I wished that Glory and I would be friends forever.

As we made our way into the hallway, a sea of kids flowed around us, back to lockers, back to class, and another sea moved toward us, toward second-lunch. Glory said she was too busy to walk with me to my next class. "Thanks so much for volunteering your house for our next meeting, Berry," she said, and she sounded like she meant it.

"No problem," I said. Big problem.

A skinny version of Glory wearing a faded flowered dress bumped arms with Glory. "Watch where you're going, Meghan!" cried Glory, clearly irritated with the girl. Meghan's eyes darted from Glory to me.

"Sorry," Meghan mumbled. "I'm late."

"You're always in the way!" said Glory. Glory didn't even see Meghan for who she was, but I did. Meghan was like me. Her eyes were a dead giveaway. There was something old in them, something weary, even something wise. Meghan looked at me, and she saw me, really saw me. Our eyes locked for a moment, and then she was gone, hurrying down the hallway.

Well, fine. I had friends. And if my friends didn't like Meghan, then neither did I.

* * *

At the dinner table, I told everyone about my momentous day. Mama wore her work clothes, a new suit she had bought at the Value Village. She'd had a momentous day, too. She had a job in an office at the University of Georgia in Athens. She thought she might be able to keep it, thought it might last a long time. We tapped our spoons against our glasses to celebrate.

Daddy kept saying, "How 'bout that?" to everything Mama and I said. I was so glad for his enthusiasm. He had made Hamburger Helper with a can of tuna, and Mama had brought home an extravagance—a bagged salad from the Kroger. We all drank milk, too. Henry gurgled in his high chair and chewed on his bib.

"So you've got friends already, Berry!" said Mama. She smiled a tired smile.

"They can't come over here," I said.

"I know how you feel, believe me," said Mama. "But this is your life, Berry. It is what it is, and true friends will understand."

"No, they won't!" I said. "They'd send *me* a turkey dinner if they really knew me!"

Henry made a face and filled his diaper. The room took on a putrid smell.

"Uh-oh," said Daddy. Mama put down her fork and ever-so-gently covered her face with her hands.

And that's when someone knocked at our door.

We all looked at one another.

"I wish it was Ed McMahon," said Mama. "I wish we'd just won the Publishers Clearing House sweepstakes. No, even better, I wish it was the doctors of heaven, here to say that your father was about to make a great breakthrough." I had never heard Mama talk like this. I knew that she meant it.

"You wished, Mama," I whispered.

"I did," she whispered back to me. "Sometimes it feels good to wish, doesn't it?"

I nodded.

Mama put her hands on either side of my face and kissed my forehead.

The knocking came again.

"I'll get it," I said.

At the door was a face I'd seen just hours before.

"Hi. I'm Meghan." She still wore the faded flowered dress. It had flowy long sleeves. She stood on the stoop looking like a ghost in the glowing light from the Scarlett O'Hara Mobile Home Park billboard beside the highway.

My heart fluttered in my throat. "I know who you are," I said. Meghan fidgeted. Was she waiting for an invitation? How did she find me here?

"I'm Berry," I said. I didn't point to my hair.

"That's a nice name," Meghan said.

I looked beyond Meghan, into the dirt front yard. No car except ours.

"Can I come in?" she said.

"Sure," I said. But I didn't mean it. I opened the screen door.

Mama was next to me. "Do you want some supper, Meghan?"

"This is my mom," I told Meghan.

"No, ma'am," said Meghan. "I ate."

Daddy appeared at the door with Henry in his arms. "I'm going to change this smelly diaper!"

"Good thinking, Marshall," said my mother. She smiled at Meghan.

"I saw your yellow car at school today," said Meghan.

"Ah," said Mama. "The car!" She began to clear the table.

"And here it is," said Meghan, "right here in the trailer park. I live in the next row over."

I stalked out the front door, and Meghan followed me. I stumped around the trailer and into the weedy backyard where crickets jumped out of my way and katydids called from the pines. Meghan followed me. She stood behind me and spoke in an even voice.

"They sent me a Thanksgiving dinner last year," she said.

I wheeled to face her.

She went on. "They asked me to come to lunch with them. They said they needed my help, they got my address, and then they sent me a Thanksgiving dinner."

My heart pounded hard in my chest as I thought about Jennifer taking my banana, Jake fetching his chocolate milk, no one wanting to know about me, no one really seeing me. Even Xavier? I thought Xavier saw me.

Meghan took a breath. "They never said another word to me after that. They didn't include me in anything. They just wanted to do their good deed. They just wanted to say they were good people."

"They *are* good!" I burst out. I couldn't help it. "They want me to help them!"

Tears filled Meghan's eyes. "They don't know," she said. She pressed her fingers to her cheeks and wiped the tears from her face. "They just don't know."

"Don't know what?"

Meghan licked her lips. "They don't know that one free Thanksgiving dinner doesn't fix anything."

I felt my own tears, then. But I didn't want to let it go. "They're good," I said.

"Yeah," said Meghan. "They're good. But they won't know you. And what you don't know is that there are lots of kids in that school who will want to know you, and I'm one of them."

I looked up into the same sky I'd wished on the night before and found the first star. "Star light, star bright," I whispered. It made me cry, and I didn't care.

"First star I see tonight," said Meghan.

The November night was chilly, and I wrapped my arms around myself. I couldn't lie to this Meghan. I didn't have to. I had nothing to tell her that she didn't already know. But she had something to tell me.

"I wished for you," Meghan said. "My mama says wishes don't come true, but I don't believe that, because here you are."

I wiped my eyes with the back of my sweatered arm and looked hard at Meghan.

"Really?" I said. And I didn't grin like a stupid possum. I just tried not to cry more.

"Really," said Meghan. "My mama says true friends are so rare, they're like finding a needle in a haystack, and I believe that. I've been wishing for a long time."

I licked my lips and thought about Flowery Branch and Lupe and all the friends I had left behind a year ago. I thought about Mama's new job and her happiness about it. I thought about Daddy's brain, so damaged and so loving and so full of hope and good humor. And I thought about myself. I needed a friend. I had wished for one. And here she stood. If I would have her.

"Do you like Johnny Depp?" I asked.

"He's the best," said Meghan.

I smiled, then.

"Dots or Jujubes?" said Meghan.

I blinked. Then I stood up straight and said, "Dots, definitely."

"Good," said Meghan.

"Good," I said.

Venus or Jupiter?

*Star light, star bright.*

# Gail Carson Levine

Gail Carson Levine started writing in elementary school when she was president of the Scribble Scrabble Club. These days she retells fairy tales and makes up some of her own. Her *Princess Tales* includes tales as familiar as "The Princess and the Pea" and as little known as "Puddocky." Although her historical novel *Dave at Night* isn't a fairy tale, its hero loses a shoe at a critical moment.

Gail's latest novel, *Fairest*, takes place in the world of *Ella Enchanted* and is a new spin on "Snow White." *Writing Magic* is a how-to book about creating exciting stories.

Gail and her husband, David, and their Airedale, Baxter, live in a 216-year-old farmhouse in upstate New York. Gail has dozens of wishes! One is to spend a day as Baxter. She'd love to discover how a dog thinks and what he takes in with his powerful sense of smell!

# Louise Hawes

Louise Hawes, who lives in North Carolina, has written books for readers of all ages. Her young-adult novels include *The Vanishing Point*, named one of the Young Adult Library Services Association's (YALSA) top 100 books for 2006, and a New York Public Library Best Book for the Teen Age; *Waiting for Christopher*, a 2003 New York Public Library Best Book for the Teen Age; and *Rosey in the Present Tense*, a 2002 YALSA Popular Paperback and a South Carolina Young People's Read. Louise, who published her first picture book, *Muti's Necklace*, in 2006, has written short fiction for several YA anthologies and a story collection for adults, *Anteaters Don't Dream* (2007). She teaches in the MFA in Writing Program at Spalding University and hopes her story and the others in this volume show readers that daydreams and wishes are good for the soul!

You can learn more about Louise and her writing at www.louisehawes.com.

# Andrea Davis Pinkney

Andrea Davis Pinkney writes:

"Oh, how I love to wish! When I was in middle school, I wished that someday I would marry a man who loved me and that we would have a daughter named Chloe. That wish came true! (I later wished for a son—another wish granted.) My daughter is now in middle school, and she helped me write my story.

"I've also wished for a wardrobe of designer clothes and for a baby pig. These wishes have not come true, though I do own a real Louis Vuitton satchel. I'm still wishing for a pig!

"One of my biggest wishes continues to come true—that I am a published author. I have written more than twenty books, including *Let It Shine: Stories of Black Women Freedom Fighters*, winner of the Coretta Scott King Honor Award and a Carter G. Woodson Honor Book; and *Duke Ellington*, a Caldecott Honor Book and a Coretta Scott King Honor Book.

"I live in New York City with my husband and frequent collaborator, illustrator Brian Pinkney, and our two children, Chloe and Dobbin."

# Liz Rosenberg

Liz Rosenberg is the author of more than twenty books for young readers, and her work has won an International Reading Association (IRA) Choice Award, the Lee Bennett Hopkins Prize, the Claudia Lewis Prize, the Paterson Prize, and other honors. One picture book, *The Carousel*, was featured on *Reading Rainbow*. She was chair of the National Book Awards for Young People's Literature in 2005, and a documentary was made about her work by First Light Productions. She is also a poet and novelist who teaches English at the State University of New York at Binghamton, where she lives with her family and two dogs. She has never stopped wishing, and she never will, even though most of her wishes have already come true.

# Patricia McCormick

Patricia McCormick was raised in Camp Hill, Pennsylvania, a nice, all-American suburb where her father was an accountant and her mother was a stay-at-home mom. She had three significantly younger sisters who formed their own little tribe, while she hid out in the basement writing short stories, being morose and moody and dreaming of living in New York City, where she now lives with her husband and son.

Her first book, *Cut*, was named an American Library Association (ALA) Best Book for Young Adults, and her latest book, *Sold*, was a National Book Award finalist.

"At a certain point," she says, "you look at your mom or dad and wonder if you could possibly have anything in common with these people who supposedly brought you into the world. I say supposedly because all any of us knows about our birth is what our parents have told us. We take it on faith. That's what this story is about: having that faith shaken—and restored."

# Catherine Stine

Catherine Stine writes:

"I'll reveal my sixth-grade secrets. I was a tall girl with a crush on a short boy. I was the 'cool artist' but wanted to be known for my writing. I was athletic but also liked being a 'girlie girl.' Now you see where I got my ideas for 'The Fashion Contest.'

"I grew up in Philadelphia and can't remember a time when I wasn't making up stories and illustrating them. I attended art school in Boston and then studied writing in New York City at the New School, where I now teach.

"I ghostwrote my first book, *The End of the Race*, about greyhound racing, for the American Girl series. (Ghostwriting isn't writing in a haunted house; it's writing under a different name.)

"Next, I wrote *Refugees*, about the friendship between an Afghan boy and an American girl. It was chosen by the New York Public Library as a Best Book for the Teen Age!

"See what's new, including the costumes in my story, at www.catherinestine.com."

# Rachel Vail

Rachel Vail is the author of many award-winning books, including the picture book *Sometimes I'm Bombaloo*; the chapter-book series Mama Rex & T; the teen series The Friendship Ring; and teen novels *Never Mind!* (cowritten with Avi), *If We Kiss*, and *You, Maybe*.

Rachel says: "The two main characters in this short story have been living in my imagination for years. They first appeared in my novel *Do-Over*, and then came back, a few years later, in my short story 'Going Sentimental' (published in the collection *Places I Never Meant to Be*, edited by Judy Blume). These two just keep demanding to have their stories told. Because it is clear to me that I will love both Jodie and Mackey until the day I die, it is one of the delights of my career to oblige them."

Rachel invites you to visit her Web site: www.RachelVail.com.

# Jane Yolen and Heidi E. Y. Stemple

Jane Yolen and her writer daughter, Heidi E. Y. Stemple, have written thirteen books together, three of which are still to come out. They are working on more.

Some things to know about each of them.

Heidi has two daughters and a cat. The older daughter recently graduated from college, the younger is about to start middle school. They all live in a house called Owl Cottage. When Heidi isn't writing or working as a personal assistant to Jane Yolen, she is a wonderful cook, a fair knitter, an avid reader, and a chauffeur, driving her younger daughter to school, to fencing, and to ballet classes and rehearsals.

Jane has three children and six grandchildren. She lives in an old farmhouse called Phoenix Farm, right next to Owl Cottage. When she isn't writing, she is reading, antiquing, calling friends, going to meetings, giving speeches, and trying desperately to get her office in order.

# A. LaFaye

Alexandria LaFaye writes:

"When my sixth-grade teacher, Mr. Magee, told my whole English class that there was a kid who was talented enough to be a published author, I wished I could become one myself. And when it turned out he was talking about me, I did! It took years and years to make my wish come true, but I kept that wish in my heart, and it inspired me to keep going. Since then, I've published a handful of books, including *The Year of the Sawdust Man*; *Nissa's Place*; *Strawberry Hill*; *Dad, in Spirit*; *Edith Shay*; and a serialized novel called *Up River*. My most recent book, *Worth*, won the Scott O'Dell Award for Historical Fiction, which was a wish come true, indeed. I hope my story and the others in this collection lead to grand wishes that come true for you all!

"If you wish to know more about me or my work, visit my Web site at www.alafaye.com."

# Deborah Wiles

Deborah Wiles writes:

"My mother taught me to wish upon the first star at night. I wished for my heart's desire. When I was in the fifth grade, I wished for Tom West to fall in love with me. I wished for Jeannie Martin to be my best friend again. I wished I would be pretty when I grew up. I even wished for world peace. I did a lot of wishing.

"When I wrote this story, I wanted to remember what it was like to want to belong so badly, to wish for a friend so deeply, and to be loved by a mother so completely.

"Today I wish to keep writing books such as *Love, Ruby Lavender*, and *Each Little Bird that Sings*, and *The Aurora County All Stars*. I wish for readers. I wish for world peace. I still wish for my heart's desire . . . and I still wish upon that first star light, star bright."

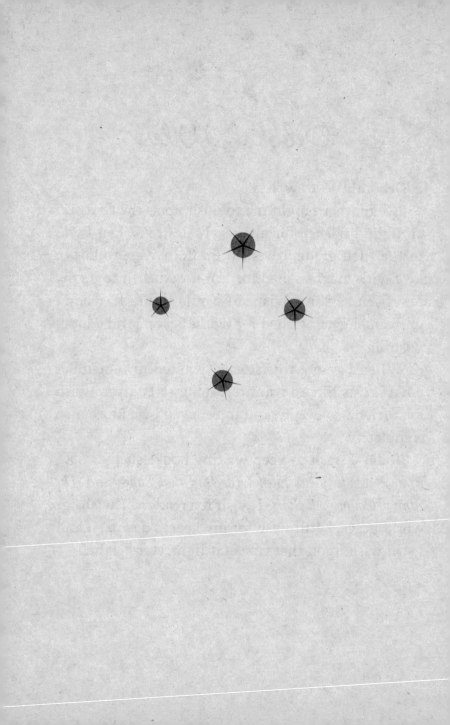

Dear Reader,

What are *your* wishes?

1. _____
_____
_____
_____
_____
_____
_____

2. _____
_____
_____
_____
_____
_____
_____

3. _____
_____
_____
_____
_____
_____
_____